PLAY

TAYLOR HART

MW01258023

COPYRIGHT INFORMATION

All rights reserved.

© 2015 ArchStone Ink

No part of this publication may be reproduced, distributed, or transmitted in any form or by any means, or stored in a database or retrieval system, without the prior permission of the publisher. The only exception is brief quotations in printed reviews. The reproduction or utilization of this work in whole or in part in any form whether electronic, mechanical or other means, known or hereafter invented, including xerography, photocopying and recording, or in any information storage or retrieval system, is forbidden without the written consent of the publisher and/or author. Thank you for respecting the hard work of this author. This edition is published by ArchStone Ink LLC.

First eBook Edition: 2015

This is a work of fiction. Names, characters, places and incidents are either the creation of the author's imagination or are used fictitiously, and any resemblance to actual persons, living or dead, business establishments, events or locales is entirely coincidental.

DEDICATION:

To my hubby – you'll always be my last play!

CONTENTS

CHAPTER 1

WHEN ROMAN YOUNG, THE DALLAS DESTROYER'S quarterback, boarded the flight to Salt Lake, he kept his hoodie on, not wanting to be recognized at the moment, which was unusual for him. He was just settling into first class when his phone buzzed.

"What?"

"Dude, you can't leave." Jake, his long-time agent and friend, spoke with clipped words. "Your team just won the championship game and there are a bunch of parties and photo ops."

Roman stared at the shiny new ring on his finger and cringed. It should have been him out there, throwing the winning touchdown, but the coaches had refused, saying they wouldn't risk his knee. He frowned. His knee was fine now. Better than fine. "I'll be back in a couple days."

Jake hesitated and then let out a long, irritated sigh. "Has Sheena roped you into something?"

Roman's breath hitched at the sound of his ex-wife's name. "No, it's not Sheena. It's…my uncle."

"Who?" Jake's voice had a sharp edge to it.

Clutching his fist, Roman let out a whiff of breath. "He passed away two weeks ago, but the attorney was told not to contact me until after the championship game."

Jake sighed. "Oh man, I'm sorry."

He unclenched his fist, seething. "It's...fine."

"You've had a rough couple of months."

Leave it to Jake to point out the obvious. "I've gotta go."

"Wait!"

"I'm not in the mood."

"Hey, did you see the headlines today?"

He'd purposely not picked up a paper or opened up his news app today. The last thing he needed to see was Sam Dumont's cheating face on the front page—with his cheating ex-wife at his side. "Can't say I have."

A soft moan escaped Jake. "No wonder you're so bugged."

"I'm bugged because my uncle died." Which, to Roman's surprise, was actually the truth.

"I know. I know. But, the owners put out a statement that they still haven't decided if you or Dumont will be their starter for next season."

That got his attention. "Even after the game?" The game where Dumont had risen to the challenge of being starting quarterback and taken the Destroyers to a championship game victory?

Jake laughed. "Right."

The ache in his chest eased a bit.

"I guess they attribute most of the team building of the last few years to you. They said it was your leadership that got them to this point and they think your knee injury is temporary."

Relief surged into him. "'Bout time they realized it."

"Ahh," Jake let out a sigh. "There's the cocky ego maniac I know and love. You've been absent lately."

Roman tugged back his hoodie and motioned to the pretty flight attendant. "Could I have some Pierre water please?"

"So why don't you hop off that plane and come to my office. We'll talk strategy."

Roman hesitated, the previous relief instantly evaporating. "I can't."

"Roman, you can't do anything crazy. I need you back for the meeting with the owners in four days."

"I won't do anything crazy." His mind flashed to four months ago, the night he'd been charged with a DUI after swerving into the other lane and hitting a woman and her son. He took the water from the flight attendant and nodded. He'd never been a drunk before, but after that night, when the woman and child had walked away with minimal injuries that could have been much worse, he'd vowed he'd never drink again. His uncle had been the one to re-focus him. He pressed a hand to his forehead and squeezed. He had to stay focused. This could be a new beginning. "Don't worry, I won't blow my chance. I'll be back."

Jake let out a low whistle. "Okay, but keep your head down and stay out of the headlines. We need to have the owners completely convinced that Roman Young is ready to take his rightful place leading the team next season."

"I'll be back in a day or two tops."

"I'm holding you to it. You're not the only one that gets a windfall when you sign a contract." He let out a whoop. "Back to the top, Roman Young..... that's where you're headed."

Roman leaned back into the chair and closed his eyes. The whirlwind of his football career flashed before his eyes. After graduating from T & M he'd gone straight to the Destroyers, touted as the top draft pick that year. The Destroyers had paid big for Roman Young, and he'd paid out for them—in spades. He'd taken them to the top and won it for them for three consecutive years. He had felt unstoppable during that time. It was like nothing could go wrong. He'd been the sweetheart of the media and the whole state of Texas.

He'd met Sheena, his ex-wife, at one of the highbrow parties that football players go to and where there are lots of women. Especially the crazy kind.

Roman had always liked women, but he'd only ever had one girlfriend all through college. The funny thing was that when he'd signed on to the Destroyers, she'd dumped him. She'd told him that she didn't like the person he was becoming.

How could she not like that he was becoming freaking rich? That's what he was becoming. His ex-wife, Sheena, had completely liked that part of him. It didn't hurt that she had been five-foot-ten and building her modeling career. Blonde, curves in all the right places. She'd been perfect. At least, he'd thought everything was perfect. The romance had been hot and heavy. He'd found himself saying "I do" three months later on a Malibu beach surrounded by his team.

Thinking of the wedding brought him back to his Uncle Jim. He gripped the certified letter in his hand, the one containing his uncle's will, and opened it. Uncle Jim had been at his wedding. He'd come to the big, white-tented reception complete with a custom-made dance floor for the beach and white lights. Sheena wanted a very public, very well attended wedding. The best designers planned everything from her dress down to the specialty-made napkins. And Sheena had looked beautiful in her sequined, snug, white dress.

Uncle Jim had stuck out like a sore thumb wearing his boots, his ranch hat, and his belt buckle. Roman had been so happy to see him. His uncle was the one who had really made his whole football career possible. After his dad had left, his mother couldn't afford all the fees required to play football in Texas, so his uncle had paid for it. When Roman's mother had died during his Junior year of college, it had been Uncle Jim who had come and insisted he pay to bury her. It had been Uncle Jim who had held Roman at the cemetery. And Uncle Jim had been the first one Roman had called when he'd found out the Destroyers wanted him.

At the wedding, Jim had pulled him into a hug and told him how proud of him he was. Tears had pooled in his eyes. It had been the best moment of Roman's life.

Then Sheena had whisked over, met his uncle, and pulled him away, saying that they needed to 'work' the event.

Looking back, Roman didn't know exactly when he felt like he'd lost himself. It had all been a blur. The media. The team. Their marriage. The society events that Sheena always insisted they needed to be at to build their 'brand.'

He clutched the will in his hand. At the final bit of advice from his Uncle. The Uncle that he'd failed to be there for. 'Roman, always remember that life's not about what you can do. It's about who you are.'

What did that even mean? For some insane reason moisture rushed to his eyes, but he blinked it back. He'd missed it. The funeral. The burial. All of it. How could the attorney not have contacted him? It was just...wrong.

He leaned back into the seat and thought about the past six months. Everything had gone to complete crap. It had started when he'd gotten sacked and dislocated his knee. That was the beginning of the end of his fairytale life. The next blow had come after the surgery, just when he'd begun insane amounts of therapy. He'd come home early one day and caught Sheena in the act. In their bed. With none other than his temporary replacement as quarterback, Dumont. Apparently Dumont had decided to be his back up off the field as well.

After clearing his throat and watching both of them scramble for their clothes, he'd realized he was shocked, but not surprised. He hadn't even known until that moment that there is a difference between those two feelings.

Sheena had stood, glaring at him and then sauntered to the bathroom and said, "Well, come on Roman, you can't really expect me to hitch myself to a washed out player looking for a comeback."

Of course, he did the cliché thing. The thing that most professional football players do when faced with a potentially career-ending injury and a cheating wife ...he went to a bar. And that's where he kept going until he'd nearly killed a woman and her kid.

That had sobered him up.

He'd called Uncle Jim. They'd talked like they hadn't talked for three years. About Sheena. About the injury. About the accident.

Uncle Jim had been a lifeline when he'd been in a dark, dark place.

Self-hate and regret coursed through him. He hadn't asked about Uncle Jim once in that whole conversation. He hadn't asked how he was doing. He didn't even know until yesterday that Uncle Jim had been in the midst of his own battle—fighting for his life.

He clutched the will and read the final lines of his uncle's message. "Roman, I don't know if you remember your trip to Wolfe Creek very well, but I am giving you the inn because I know it was a place that I felt the closest to you and your mom for those two summers. It needs some work, and I understand if you want to sell it and be done, but I'm not letting you off the hook that easily."

Roman had booked his ticket last night. He'd also contacted the attorney, Robert Burcher, in charge of his uncle's estate and ripped him for not letting him know about the funeral. Then he told him he wanted to sell the place immediately. Burcher had told him that he already had a buyer in place. The paperwork just needed to be signed—in person and at the inn, according to his uncle's wishes.

He clutched the thick stationary. Why hadn't his uncle wanted him to go to the funeral? And what did his uncle think he would want with an inn anyway?

Roman stepped out of the airport and immediately cursed himself for not thinking about the weather. He hadn't expected to be standing in the freezing cold as he tried catching a cab outside of the Salt Lake City airport. He hunched even further into his thin hoodie as he slipped into the cab. "Wolfe Creek."

The cab driver turned back and frowned. "Wolfe Creek, up past Ogden?"

Roman couldn't remember how long it took to get from Salt Lake City to Wolfe Creek, he'd only been twelve and thirteen during those visits. "Something the matter with that?"

The driver lifted his eyebrows and laughed, pointing out the window. "Have you seen this snow? It hasn't snowed like this in a long, long time, and that canyon will be nasty."

Roman sighed and pulled a hundred dollar bill out of his wallet. "Look, if you take me up there, this your tip."

The cab driver hesitated and then snatched the money and shook his head. He was older, and his grey-flecked black hair stuck out of a beanie cap. "Okay, I'll take you, but you're paying for both ways, and I need to see another one of these when we get there."

"Fine." Roman held his hands up to intercept the warm air from the vents. "Just turn up the heat."

Rush hour traffic was thick and slow and an hour later, the driver finally turned off the freeway and headed into Ogden.

Roman watched the heavy snow falling on everything and everyone. The plows were out in full force. Roman listened to the radio that cab driver had on, telling people to stay inside, this was the next big one. People drove slowly. They passed an accident going through town and had to wait twenty minutes to be re-routed. "How much longer up the canyon?"

The cab driver turned and gave him a slow smile. "Why? Are you losing your nerve now?"

The fact that he *was* kind of doubting how they would get up there made him keep his mouth shut.

The cab driver laughed. "Look, it's another twenty minutes on a good day, I guess it'll probably be an hour before we get up there in all this snow … if we get up there."

"What do you mean 'if?'"

The cab driver motioned to the road. "What do you mean, what do I mean? This is the Rocky Mountains."

Roman frowned. "Right."

The cab driver looked back and laughed. "You've never been snowed in? Where are you from?"

The pit of Roman's gut clenched. He couldn't get snowed in up here. He had to be at the meeting with the team owners. "Texas."

"Ahh." The cab driver made it through town and started up the canyon on a two-lane road. "I hope you have family up here or know someone because you're going to be up here for a couple of days."

Flashing lights ahead showed a diesel truck off to the side of the road. Roman cringed. "Can you turn back?"

The cab driver slowed. "I could try to pull over and turn back if you want. You could probably at least get a hotel in Ogden."

His uncle's face flashed through his mind. "Never mind, just keep going. There's something I have to do."

The cab driver tsked his tongue. "Man, she must be pretty good looking."

An unwilling laugh rolled out of him. "No, I'm not going up there for a woman."

The cab driver let out a muffled laugh. "Cold and lonely, that's a bad combination."

The Alaskan Inn looked exactly as he remembered it. Two stories, stone around the foundation and long, round logs framed the exterior. It was definitely a rustic cabin. Somehow, it was clearly visible through the still falling snow. Roman remembered it being large and cozy, but he didn't remember the big pine trees that stood guard next to it. He didn't remember the turn around driveway that was, amazingly, plowed. He definitely didn't remember white lights being hung around it, making it look like something out of a cheesy Christmas movie, well, except for a couple of lights that had burnt out.

The cab driver pulled in front of the inn and sighed. "That'll be eight-hundred dollars, plus tip."

Roman scoffed, "What?"

He motioned to the outside. "I've risked life and limb to get you up here, and I think you can pay it … Roman Young."

Ahh. Of course. The driver had recognized who he was even though he'd kept his hoodie on the whole time in the cab. He looked into the rearview mirror and met the smirking face of the driver. "Really?"

He put his hand out. "I'll charge it nice and neat to your credit card. Let's make it a cool thousand with tip, and then you won't have to worry about the media showing up."

Roman rolled his eyes but relented, passing his card up to him. It had not been a good idea to come today. It was bad timing, risky to his career and physically dangerous in this weather. Add in the personal conflict, and no, he definitely didn't want any media attention right now. "Okay, but if you leak this, I'm suing."

The cab driver ran his card and handed it back. "Leak what? I don't know what you're talking about."

Roman rolled his eyes and got out of the car. "I mean it." The last thing he needed was to have a news crew show up. His Uncle Jim hated the media. From the very start he'd told Roman that he'd do well to keep his nose clean and keep a low profile, but Roman hadn't listened to him then. Regrettably, he'd listened to Sheena and her strategy for taking them both to the top.

Even though the outside was lit up and the driveway was clear, it didn't look like anybody was home. It was completely dark. Roman held the door of the cab open. "Can you hold on and take me to a hotel if no one's here?"

But the cab driver took off with a jerk, slammed the door shut with the momentum, and yelled out the window, "Good luck, but this ride has to get back to the city before they shut down the roads. Thanks for the tip!"

Roman watched him go and irritation coursed through him. Snow was already gathered on the tip of his nose. He turned back and instantly the twinkle lights blinked out. He turned in a quick circle. The light that lit up the road had gone out, too. "Perfect." He trudged toward the front door, taking care not to slip. He dug into his pocket and pulled out the envelope. He tipped it upside down, letting the key fall into his hand. He put it into the door and eased it open.

The first thing he noticed, other than the fact that it was very dark, was that the inside was cold, too. He put his suitcase down and tried to remember anything from those two trips about where furniture would be. Nothing. He pulled out his cell phone and pulled up the flashlight app. Two seconds later, his phone died.

He'd been playing games on his phone during the whole flight. He growled and stuffed it back into his pocket. He had to rely on the small amount of light from the moon to make out the furniture and navigate toward the fireplace.

He felt for a switch to light it, hoping a nice gas fireplace would instantly light. No such luck. But he did find a box of matches!

After sliding it open, his heart plunged—the box was empty. He cursed and banged his fist against the side of the fireplace. "Seriously?"

Roman sucked in a long breath and tried to get his frustration under control. He felt like he was trying to throw a pass for a first down with no open receivers. "Uncle Jim!" He yelled and spun around, looking for anything that could be used for fuel.

He stumbled around, feeling the walls, trying to find the way to the kitchen. He needed to get in there, turn on a light and find some matches.

Part of a wall gave, and he pushed a door into the kitchen. He felt along the side of the wall and found a light switch. He flipped it.

Nothing.

He flipped it quickly back and forth and felt for another one. "Man!"

Keeping his hand against the wall, he felt his way around, hoping he could find the cupboards and rummage for something. Soft light poured in from the outside windows of the kitchen. The moon shone high in the sky, visible even through the snow that fell in fluffy clumps. The whole scene looked like something out of a storybook—all soft, cozy, and white. Well, minus the warm part of cozy. The very important warm part that propelled him to go to the massive cupboards and fling them open, searching for something helpful.

He thought he saw a box of matches and reached up, extending himself as far as he could to get the box, thinking that whoever usually got into these top cupboards must be a giant.

The box stayed just out of reach. It seemed like every time he almost touched it the box scooted back, evading him.

Without warning, the kitchen door burst open, and even colder air rushed through the room.

"Who's there? Show yourself!" Roman tried to get a view of this person.

The sound of a shotgun being cocked put him on alert. Then the barrel of a shotgun came into view. His heart rate spiked. "Put the gun down," he said calmly.

If he'd anticipated the assailant would calmly put the shotgun down, he'd been half right. The shotgun fell to the ground and the intruder ran straight for him, getting in a good shove to Roman's ribs and knocking him off balance. He stumbled back and then tripped over a chair and fell.

At this point, all Roman knew was this guy would pay.

The assailant pounced on him, taking him all the way to the floor.

Roman was grateful he'd trained so hard to get his strength and agility back. He easily used his opponent's momentum to roll them both. He stopped when he was on top and quickly secured both his assailant's hands above his head, noting he wasn't very big, even in all the snow gear he had on. "Mess with the bull, get the horn."

"Ouch!"

As the adrenaline faded, Roman realized the body he was currently subduing was definitely feminine. He reacted as if he'd bit into a piece of cake expecting chocolate and realizing it was salt cake instead.

Immediately he yanked back his hold, pulling himself up. "What the—"

"Language." The woman stood up quickly and gave him a look that told him she wished she still had the shotgun. She reached for something and then flipped on a lantern flashlight.

The first thing he noticed, besides the fact that she looked angry, was that her eyes were green. Cat green, as his mother would have said. His mother had been a cat fan. He'd often teased her about being the cat lady, but he'd brought her every stray kitten he'd found toward the end of the cancer, hoping something would cheer her up.

Red hair with soft curls tumbled down her shoulders. It was the color of leaves turning in the fall. He almost couldn't breathe for a second. She looked so beautiful and fierce and like she would rip his head off if she could. He'd seen that kind of ferocity in only a few people—cancer survivors and three-hundred pound defensive tackles that were getting paid a heck of a lot of money to put him on his backside. For no good reason, it made him laugh.

It was evidently the wrong response. It made her ferocity increase. He could tell from the way her cat-green eyes narrowed before she bent to pick the shotgun up. "I wouldn't laugh."

He stuck his hand out. "Whoa. I think we've had enough of the gun for tonight, don't you?"

"Who are you?" She used both hands to brace the shotgun against her shoulder and she placed one foot behind her as if she were preparing to fire.

If only there had been more time to truly appreciate the mussed up, angry, and still beautiful woman in front of him. "Look, just relax?"

This time she smirked, actually smirked, at him. "Excuse me, who do you think you are? I can have the cops here in two seconds." She switched her stance and put the shotgun down and propped it against the table. She pulled out a phone.

The commanding way she said it, like some prison warden, made him laugh again.

With her thumb, she swiped the screen on her phone and pushed in a code. "Apparently you like to go around breaking into people's places. What? Did you hear about Jim and think you could come squat here or something?" A horrid look washed over her face. She pinched her lips. "Well, you can't." She pressed a button and put the phone to her ear, pinching her lips in satisfaction.

On reflex, he took her phone away from her and pushed end. He didn't need this kind of publicity for breaking and entering at the moment. His agent definitely wouldn't be happy about something like that. "Now, hold on."

Nails scraped his hand as she tried to retrieve what he'd taken. "Hey!"

Altering his stance, he held the phone out of reach. "I said hold on." Apparently, she wasn't really going to kill him, so that was a relief.

Relentless was what he would call her antics for getting the phone back. "Give me my phone!"

It wasn't that he thought she was dangerous or that she wasn't owed an explanation, but the aggressive way she reached for her phone made him want to keep it. He easily faked right and dodged left.

She fell fast. She'd clearly planned on the weight of his body to ram against but ended up landing on the floor instead.

It struck him that he was acting like a teenager. She clearly knew his uncle and was just trying to protect his property. "I'm sorry," he said it quickly, but sincerely. He reached a hand out to help her up.

The woman scowled at his hand and stood by herself. She sucked in a long gulp of air, plucking her phone out of his hand. "You better tell me who you are and what you want." Her eyes were on fire. He couldn't help thinking it matched her hair.

He let out a breath and held back a laugh. "I'm the owner."

The words hung in the air, and she studied him for a second, examining him the way he would examine a new play that coach had added to the playbook. Intensely. Carefully.

"You're Jim's nephew?" It wasn't as much a statement as something that came out of her mouth with as much mystifying power as he felt. She looked him up and down, this time her eyes going into slits. "The great Roman Young."

This time, he did laugh. "Guess that description's accurate." He couldn't say he didn't like the way 'great' sounded in front of his name.

Without warning she laughed, hard and without humor. She shook her head and picked up the shotgun, putting it behind the kitchen door. "Selfish. Selfish. Selfish."

He was confused. "What?"

She tsked her tongue. "Of course you don't want me to call the police with the media coverage you've had lately." She shuffled to the same cupboard he'd searched earlier and whipped it open, pulling out a box of matches. "Do you know how many things need to get done around here? How many times I've had to run over here to keep the riffraff out at night and check stuff? Do you have *any* idea how much needs to be done before people can stay here, and we're supposed to be opening in two months?" She shook her head and held up the box of matches. Her expression shifted from anger to exasperation. "Seriously, why didn't you start a fire? It's cold in here."

He ran his hand over the stubble on his face. Before he could move to help, she had already walked into the main room and was making noise. He followed and watched as she expertly built a fire, trying to blow off her little rant about his selfishness. People never understood him. "I couldn't find a switch or matches." The belated reply to her belittling observation about the fire sounded lame, even to him.

She whipped her head back. The red curls and her green eyes looked enchanting backlit by the flame. She grinned, and, at that point, he knew she was every bit as bewitching as he'd first thought, but not at all helpless. "The power's out, genius. Oh, and don't worry. I won't tell anyone you beat up on a girl."

Awkward. After all, what was she? He cocked his head and sized her up. Probably five foot eight, definitely slight of frame. Underneath that snowsuit he couldn't imagine her being too big. Without thinking, he checked her left hand. Checked the finger that would matter. For some reason, he was disappointed that a band encircled it. "Sorry." He meant it.

She laughed, and this time it was rich and wonderful. He told himself to stop even thinking about her laugh.

"Jim's nephew." She shook her head. "Wow. I mean, I knew you owned the place, but I … Jim said you weren't the kind that would come. He said I'd probably have to communicate via email." She grimaced and moved for a small closet off of the main doors. "Well, I have to go." She tugged out a sleeping bag. "Power's off. Here's a sleeping bag. You'll have to sleep on the floor in front of the fire tonight if you want to keep warm." She tossed it at his feet and then paused.

He couldn't believe this. "What do you mean? Won't the power come back on soon?"

She took off toward the kitchen, waving him back with her. "Uh—don't hold your breath." She walked through the swivel kitchen door and he followed. She picked up a piece of paper off the table and shoved it at his chest, taking a match and lighting another lantern. "Good thing you're here, here's a list of all the stuff that needs to be fixed. You saved me having to email it to you." She moved to the kitchen door and threw back a grin. "I'll see you in the morning if you survive the night."

He couldn't decide if he liked her or not. He rushed to the kitchen door and threw the door wide. "Hey, isn't there a hotel or something?"

She moved for a snowmobile, but turned back. "Maybe you should have come to the funeral and you could have met someone who might be willing to help you out." Her cat-like eyes flashed wide.

He jerked back, unprepared for the direct emotional hit.

She slung her leg up and onto a snowmobile. "You *are* in a bed and breakfast."

He moved out onto the deck, ticked off, their eyes locked.

She grinned and the rip roar of the snowmobile sounded into the air. She winked at him and Roman knew it was meant to taunt him.

It worked. Anger flared inside him and he cursed. Turning back into the house, he shut the kitchen door, locked it and huffed back to the living room. Staring at the fire, he pushed open the sleeping bag, thinking that this sleeping bag was probably the same one he'd used all those years ago when his uncle had taken him camping. He rustled in his bag and found his phone charger, taking care to plug in the phone and hoping the power might come back on so it could get a charge.

He laid back on the sleeping bag, staring at the fire and shook his head. "Well, Uncle Jim, I'm here." He blinked. "But you're not here to tell me one of your ghost stories." His mind flashed, again, to the red head and the way she'd winked at him. He did not like her he decided.

Getting up, he got into the bag and begrudgingly tugged it up into place around his head. He forced himself to take in deep breaths and try to relax. He would get some sleep and then meet with the attorney tomorrow and figure out how to get this place sold. Then he would get as far away from the Alaskan Inn as he could get.

CHAPTER 2

THE NEXT MORNING ROMAN WOKE to the sound of clicking. He jerked awake, rudely brought back to the reality that he lay huddled in a sleeping bag, in yesterday's clothes, with a cold nose. Last night he'd fallen asleep ticked at the red-haired crazy woman, and he'd woken just as ticked. How dare she tell him he should have come to funeral? She knew nothing about him and his life. He hadn't even known about the funeral. Who was she to act all superior and judge him? He tried to pull the zipper back, but it had been cold last night, and he'd zipped the mummy bag as tightly as he could. He struggled for a few seconds. Then he heard the clicking again. "Hey!" he yelled. It wasn't a problem to roll to his front and maneuver himself to his feet in one core-tightening move.

Click, click, click.

He jumped toward the kitchen and the sound. "Helloo!" All he needed was another unwelcome guest. What had the crazy red head called the people she had to keep at bay last night? Riffraff? He wouldn't think this small town would have much riffraff.

Before he could get to the swiveling kitchen door, it slammed open, banging him right in the head.

He fell back, turning into a face plant as he fell. He caught himself before he hit too hard.

"Oh land sakes, what's this?" a loud voice called out.

Roman squiggled his way to his side, not knowing what to expect, and found himself staring up into the face of an older lady that looked faintly familiar.

She held a frying pan in her hand with something in it. She already had a rolling laugh coming out of her. She wore jeans and tall black boots. She had her hair pulled back into a bun at the top of her head and wire-rimmed glasses on her face. She peered down. "I heard you were here, but I didn't realize Katie had locked you up in a mummy bag." She lifted the pan. "Made you some pancakes."

The playful, yet stern look on her face didn't put Roman completely at ease. "Oh." It was all he could think of to say at the moment. "My zipper's stuck."

At this, she slapped her leg and cackled out a laugh, making a strand of hair fall out of the flimsy bun. "Well, if I had a nickel for every time I've heard a man say that." She took two steps to the table and put the pan down on a worn hot pad. "Well let's see if we can fix you up, Mr. Roman."

Mr. Roman. He flashed to being eleven and being teased about how many pancakes he could eat. "Mrs. K?" He couldn't believe he remembered that.

She bent over him, smelling of talcum powder and eggs. She pulled back and grinned, fiddling with the zipper. "That's right. That's a good boy." She winked. "Boys always remember old ladies that feed them."

While she fiddled and finally won with the zipper, he wondered exactly how old she must be. He sat up and stepped out of the sleeping bag, emerging like a snake from a skin. "You have no idea how much better that feels. Thank you."

Mrs. K only paused for a second and studied him. "Well, you've grown up, Roman." Her eyes looked him up and down, not like a woman checking him out, but more like a grandmother appraising him. It was the same way his own mother used to look at him. Then she folded him into her arms.

For a second, he didn't react, but when she didn't let go, he hugged her back. He didn't know what to say. "Er, thanks?"

With a slight crook to her walk, she moved to the table and retrieved the pancakes. "Come on, honey, let's go sit at the table and talk."

Even though he had a dietitian that watched everything he ate to ensure he got the right amounts of protein, carbs, and fat, he would definitely take her up on her pancakes. If he remembered right, Mrs. K's pancakes were something of an experience. His stomach grumbled. "I'll be right in, I just have one call to make real quick."

He retrieved his phone from the charger against the wall and pressed the attorney's number.

"Hello."

"It's Roman Young. I'm in Wolfe Creek, I need you to meet me over here sometime today and get the paperwork signed."

"Oh, dear …"

"Mr. Burcher, I need to get this done today."

"I'm sorry, Mr. Young. The roads up the canyon have closed. It looks like it'll be a couple of days."

"Days?"

He sighed. "These storms take on a mind of their own. But I promise you as soon as the roads open, I'll be there."

The kitchen looked different in the daylight. The mahogany cupboards were not as polished as he remembered. They looked worn. The large table matched the cupboards and Roman vividly remembered how much he loved this kitchen. He took in the faded apple décor, from the little curtains over the sink window to the wallpaper. But, it was still clean and tidy. Mrs. K put the pancakes down next to a steaming plate of eggs and motioned for him to sit. "It's been almost a year since I've cooked for anyone except your uncle in this kitchen." Her face turned sad. "For a long time he wanted to keep having groups of people come because he enjoyed that, you know. He enjoyed the company. He enjoyed seeing other people appreciate the amenities that Wolfe Creek has to offer: the lakes, the skiing. But this place got so run down it couldn't compete with those new developments up the hill, ya know." She heaped a pile of eggs and two pancakes onto his plate without asking him what he wanted. Syrup was dumped on the top before he could do it himself. She folded her arms. "Will you say grace, Roman?"

It hit him that it'd been roughly three years since he'd said grace. Three years since he'd been married and three years since he'd bowed his head. But, as the saying goes, 'it's like riding a bike.' The words tumbled off of his lips with the rapidity of his eleven year old self that had been hungry and wanting to take a bite of the homemade pancakes.

She sat and motioned to the papers on the table. "I see Katie gave you a list?"

Roman nodded and shoved in a bite of pancake. The taste of sugar-filled maple syrup and fluffiness melted in his mouth. "Hmm."

His phone buzzed in his pant pocket, and he reached for it, momentarily forgetting Katie's list. It was his agent, asking when he was coming back. He put his phone back and worried about the meeting with the owners. But he had three days. Surely the storm would clear by then. Resigned to the fact that he'd be stuck here for a while, he nodded to Mrs. K, thinking that there were worse places to be stuck. He remembered how the team had gotten stuck in Minnesota the last time they had played there. Granted, they had been in a nice hotel. They'd ordered up plate after plate of food, but the food hadn't been this good.

Mrs. K grinned. "Pancakes are my specialty."

"They're delicious." He grinned back and took another bite.

When Katie came in, he was looking over the list and eating his breakfast.

She ignored him and made coffee. "Hey, Mrs. K, how are you today?"

"Doing good, Katie girl, doing good." She pulled her into a half hug. "How's your guy?"

It served as a stark reminder to Roman that she was married. Trying to sneak a good look at her, without being obvious, he glanced up from his list. Her red hair lay in soft curls down to the middle of her back. She wore a puffy, black coat, but began to unzip it. As she finally turned to face him, she caught him looking.

For whatever reason, the fact she'd caught him glancing at her made him nervous. He reached for his coffee and ended up knocking it over, spilling it across the supply list. "Crap." He tried to stand too fast and knocked his thighs hard against the table, making the table jerk and the fresh syrup topple over, too.

"My heavens!" Mrs. K reached for a kitchen towel.

In a flash, Katie picked up the syrup, preventing more oozing from mixing with the coffee. She tugged the list ·away, and a line of coffee dripped from the table to the counter sink. "Think you can get out of the chores if you ruin the list?"

"Chores?" The way he said it made him sound like a teenager after his mother had demanded he mow the lawn. He didn't know why he reacted this way to this woman. He cleared his throat and used his hand to slick the coffee and syrup onto his plate. Then he used his napkin to mop up the remaining mess. "I mean, I thought that list was for supplies." He maneuvered over to the sink.

Katie waved the list over the sink. The look on her face told him that she found him amusing. "I figured you'd want to help get things done today."

He caught a glint of her ring. On her left hand. Definitely married.

"I mean," she hesitated, looking out the window, "there's nowhere to go. Even the ski resorts need to get ahold of their avalanche control precautions." She paused, licking her lips. "Are you here to ski?"

He knew that she wasn't licking her lips for any other reason than because they were probably chapped, but instantly he noticed how close they stood together. The dishes dropped into the sink. The cup he'd used for coffee broke. He jerked back.

"Land sakes!" Mrs. K exclaimed, bustling in between them and reaching in for the broken pieces. She scowled at him. "Katie, get this boy out of my kitchen, now!"

Hating himself at this moment, it wasn't like him at all to be a complete klutz, Roman got out of Mrs. K's way.

Katie covered her face and let out a small laugh. She motioned to the door. "I'd say you better get your boots and come with me!"

"Where can we go with all this snow?" At this point he wasn't sure he wanted to go anywhere with this woman. She made him slightly nervous. It had been a long time since Roman had been so on edge.

Shaking her head, Katie lifted an eyebrow. "What? Are you afraid of little old me?"

The way she said it was slightly seductive. At least, he took it as seductive, and he wasn't one to back away from a challenge. He backed out of the living room, remembering that any kind of gear was stored in the large front closet by the front door. "Getting boots."

After the door creaked open, he found an assortment of things and pulled out what looked like serious mountaineering boots. Most likely they had belonged to his uncle. He found a Carhartt coat and a Dallas Destroyers beanie cap on a hook. Emotion tugged at him as he pulled on a matching pair of gloves. He'd given these to his uncle the first year he'd signed with the team.

Trudging through the kitchen, he didn't say a word as he went for the door. He could see Katie already sitting on a snowmobile, a trailer attached to the back.

"Best behavior, young man."

Roman grinned at Mrs. K, who was washing dishes. "Ah, thank you for breakfast."

She winked at him. "Have fun."

When Roman got down the steps to Katie, she tossed her head back and grinned. "Get on the back, Quarterback."

For a second, he paused. "You knew?" The night before he was sure anyone who treated him so rudely must not know exactly who he was.

A pink pom pom beanie was on her head, complete with knitted strings that were braided down the sides over her ears. The side of her lip tugged up. "You think your uncle let anyone in this town NOT know about the great Roman Young?"

Tentatively, he got on behind her, totally bewildered and confused by the fact that—since she knew who he was—she was still treating him this way. He lightly put his hands on her hips. She had a tiny waste and he wondered, if he tightened his hold, if he could touch his fingers together.

She laughed and jolted as she took off.

He held on tighter.

She laughed again. "Sheesh, for goodness sake you won't break me, just put your arms around my waist."

They flew across the powdered-driveway. "Man, there's a lot of snow, this resembled a driveway last night."

Katie scoffed. "Wolfe Creek got about seventeen inches just last night and you know it's not supposed to let up for a while."

He frowned, thinking of Mr. Burcher. "I heard."

Leaning forward and hunching down, he was able to get a better hold. The smell of lemon assaulted him. He ducked behind her, wishing he'd worn sunglasses to block the spray of snow. He popped his head out and saw that they were on what appeared to be a main road, speeding toward a small cluster of stores that, despite the weather, had customers coming and going.

Other snowmobilers passed by. Katie waved at each of them, sometimes shouting hello. Roman was mystified that this town continued to operate as if the snow didn't matter.

They pulled into Henry's Hardware and parked next to, Roman counted, five other snowmobiles with attached trailers.

Katie cut the engine and waited for him to get off. Her eyes held a mischievous glint as she casually picked up a handful of snow and tossed it at him when she walked past. "Come on, Quarterback, haven't you ever seen a winter storm before?"

Part of the snow fell lightly against his cheek, and he felt even more confused as he followed Katie into the hardware store. Was she flirting with him? He was used to the more direct approach— like scantily clad women draping themselves along his body and sticking like plastic wrap on a glass dish. He felt off kilter with Katie.

Katie pulled off her cap and nodded towards a cart. "Do you mind pushing it? We can get supplies," she paused and pulled her phone out of a zipper pocket in the front of her own Carhartt jacket. "I figure we can finish getting carpet ripped out in the upstairs before I have to go pick up my son."

The idea that she thought he was going to rip carpet out was quickly overshadowed by the fact she'd mentioned a son. He blinked. *She's married. She's married.* He needed to quit thinking that she had some kind of attraction to him or something.

With that reminder, he grabbed a cart and jogged two steps to catch up to her.

She already had a box of nails and tossed them inside the cart. She scanned the shelves. "We also need to secure the stairs. I'm thinking we rip up the carpet and pound in the nails, see which ones are loose. Your uncle, God rest his soul, loved the place, but let's face it—he left a heck of a lot of work to be done to get it up to par." She glanced at him. "And getting it in shape before the spring crowd hits is going to be tough."

It did occur to Roman that he should probably tell her that he was just here to sign paperwork and get the place sold, but, he reasoned, with the storm he wouldn't be leaving for a day or two, and any improvements couldn't hurt the sale. Not to mention that Katie looked so happy to be planning away. Maybe he would try to get it in the contract that she could stay the caretaker, or whatever she was.

"What?" She stopped moving and looked defensive.

Had he been staring? Clearing his throat, he turned to the paint. "Nothing. Nothing." Suddenly, he noticed the Christmas music humming in the background. "What's with the music?"

Instantly, she frowned and shook her finger at him. "You just keep quiet about the music." There was a sudden edge to her tone. "Henry has enough problems to think about with Mrs. K's health and everything else right now. The music is the least of his concerns," she snapped.

That was not the reason he had expected. "What are you talking about—Mrs. K's health?" The fact that he didn't know who Henry was didn't seem to matter at the moment. "The Mrs. K that fed me pancakes today?"

Her face softened. "Yes." Moisture filled her eyes. Her green eyes shined even brighter. "Mrs. K has cancer." She shook her head. "And she told me the other day that after seeing your uncle die, she just can't believe that she can get a miracle."

The center of his chest clutched with emotion. He thought of his uncle and for some insane reason he felt his own eyes get waterywhich took him aback. He turned away from her and swallowed. Not her, too.

He heard Katie let out a soft sigh. "I'm sorry. I guess ... I guess this all rings close to home with your uncle and everything." A hand touched his shoulder. "I didn't tell you how sorry I am about Jim. He was a good man." ·

Turning back around, his eyes locked with hers and he felt a shiver of warmth move through him. Here was something that the people in his life recently had lacked—sincerity. All he could do was nod again. Jim was probably the only person he did care about, at least at this point in his life, and he was gone. "Thank you, that means a lot."

Pulling her hand back, she turned to the shelves. She took two cans of primer and plunked them into the cart, immediately reaching for two more cans of paint. "Grey is the big color right now." She cleared her throat again and flashed him a tentative smile. "I was thinking that we could accent with red pillows and white trim. Maybe some rugs that thread some deep blue into it and have some decorative shabby chic lamps and chandeliers. I think it would add a modern feeling to the cabin." She pulled the cart behind her, turning into a new aisle. She took some cabinet hardware off of the shelf. "The rustic cupboards in the kitchen can stay. I haven't decided if we should paint them white. You know, to brighten up the kitchen. I watched a YouTube video on how to actually make them look kind of antiquey by using a permanent black marker to trace the lines." She cocked her head to the side, studying an array of handles. She took a clump of them out and dropped them into the cart. "But, we will need to put hardware on either way, so let's go ahead and get these." She turned for confirmation. "Is that okay?"

All Roman knew at this moment was that he didn't want to disappoint this woman that had touched his shoulder and shown a more kind-hearted response to his uncle's death than anyone else in his life. Spending a couple of days rehabbing the cabin might not be a bad way to spend his time. Especially if he got to spend it with her. Annoyance washed over him. *Married*. He had to remember. She was married.

Her green eyes narrowed, making her look more like a 'Kat' than a 'Katie.' "What?"

"Nothing," he spit out. "What?"

Putting a hand on her hip, she moved closer to him, searching his eyes. "What I'm really asking for is budget approval."

His pulse raced, and he stepped back, trying to get as far as he could from the lemon fragrance that wafted off of her. "Sure. Absolutely. Whatever you want."

Lifting her eyebrows, she grinned. "Really? Anything I want?"

It wasn't just that his mind felt scrambled. Did the manager keep the heat up in here? He tugged off his coat. "Get all the supplies you need." He folded his coat and put it in the front part of the cart.

The way she spun on her heel and flashed a wide smile told him he was going to vehemently regret giving her that kind of a license.

She rattled on about different people they saw in the store. There was Mrs. Harper, the old school teacher. When Katie introduced him as Jim's nephew, Mrs. Harper hugged him and said how sorry she was. She proceeded to make a point of introducing her daughter who happened to be trapped in town for the weekend and suggested he might take her out. The idea that Mrs. Harper would blatantly throw her quiet daughter at him was just a bit much. Her daughter wasn't bad looking, but she seemed painfully shy in his presence so her mother's suggestion was just weird. But he'd definitely had weirder encounters with mothers wanting him to date their daughters, so he just nodded politely.

At this, Katie had promptly covered her face and pushed the cart away from them, leaving him to make excuses and describe the projects that they were knee deep in. Of course he left out the fact that he'd only really committed to doing them this morning. He walked away from the whole thing and endured more laughter and soft punches to the shoulder from Katie.

"Big quarterback's in town, ladies. It's *The Bachelor* comes to Wolfe Creek. Who will get a rose?"

Not really amused, he pretended to play along anyway. "Right, maybe instead of handing out roses, we'll give power tools to the girls that know how to overhaul the most projects around the inn."

She snapped her fingers with delight. "Exactly, and you could strut around with a tool belt on and show them how to do stuff."

He snickered. "Problem is I don't know how to do much *stuff*."

She rolled her eyes. "That's okay, QB. Throwing a ball is all you need to know how to do, right?"

Although it shouldn't really be an insult, it kind of did sound like an insult. "What does that mean?"

She kept strolling down the aisles, adding things to the cart. "Nothing." She focused on a drill. "I need a drill. Are you okay with buying this?"

The drill was not on his radar. "Yeah, whatever. What did you mean quarterbacks only have to throw a ball?"

She forced him to a stop by cutting him off as she moved to the other side of the aisle and added something else to the cart. She was frowning when she replied, "You sound offended."

"I'm not." It came out a little too quickly.

She studied him for a second then turned their cart to the check out lane. "Chill out, QB, lots of women want a man that can throw a ball." She lifted an eyebrow. "And I admit, you do that well."

Once again, the compliment sounded like an insult. "I do lots of other things well." He threw out at her.

She began unloading all the things in the check out lane. "I didn't say you don't."

Memories of his mother teaching him things flashed into his mind. "I can cook."

The side of her lip tugged up. "I'm happy for you." She pushed the cart through and nodded to the cashier.

Angrily, without knowing why he should feel angry, he tugged his card out of his wallet and didn't even look at the total, his eyes riveted on her. "Have you ever watched spring training or a football documentary on all the things we have to do to maintain ourselves?"

He signed a slip, and she was already taking some of the bungee cords out of the cart along with a tarp, moving them out into the snow.

He zipped up and trudged faster, trying to keep up with her. She smashed her pom pom hat on her head and went to the task of organizing everything on the trailer of the snow mobile. For a few seconds he wondered if she'd heard his question. "Do you know what football players go through?"

She got everything situated and gave him half of the tarp, ignoring the angst in his voice. "Actually, I've been too busy the last couple years to honestly care." She finished fastening the last strap and then held his gaze.

Roman stared back at her. For some reason, he kind of liked the way Katie treated him. Normal. She was mean to him, but he could tell this was her being normal. It probably just felt like she was being mean because most people fell all over themselves around him, he reasoned. But, he didn't think she respected him and that wasn't okay with him. Roman swiftly took the snow mobile keys out of Katie's hand. He got on first.

"Hey!" she protested, trying to reach across him and swipe the keys out of his hand.

He laughed, liking the feeling of keeping something away from her. "Oh, no!" A thought occurred to him. "Whose snow mobile is this anyway?"

A sheepish grin peeked across her face. She pointed at him. "Your uncle's."

Slipping the key into the starter, he grinned. "Exactly."

After hesitating and then crossing her arms, she lifted her brows. "Well, Quarterback, you don't always get your way." She shook her head back and forth and stomped away from him, heading toward the Lunch Lizard Diner. "I'm hungry."

Roman's heart was racing, and he wanted to take off. Fast. Just fly out of the parking lot and away from this incredibly RUDE woman, but he didn't. It had nothing to do with the fact he really didn't know what he would do with all these supplies. The snow was still flying, but they had used a tarp to cover them from it. He was torn between wanting to leave and wanting to confront her. Finally, he decided this female—married or not—needed a piece of his mind. You don't leave somebody that's new to town sitting on a snow mobile all by himself with supplies you wanted to purchase. It was just rude!

He got off the snowmobile and stalked toward Leaping Lizard Diner. Swinging the door back, he found her at a booth next to the window. An older lady in a red dress and big, black boots stood in front of her, putting down two glasses of water. He put on his severe face. The one he saved for coaches that told him his knee wasn't ready for play time. The one he saved for ex-wives who sat across from him with her attorney and demanded half of everything.

Katie saw him and gave him a huge, innocent smile and waved him over. "Lee Ann, meet Roman—Jim's nephew. The one he always talked about."

Immediately, the big boot lady, who had to be a foot and a half shorter than him, hugged him, putting her head against his side. "I loved your uncle Jim."

Once again, Roman was taken by surprise. The only thing that could have shaken him down, besides being slammed by a three hundred pound line backer, was this kind of open affection and concern. Unwanted emotion choked up his throat. He patted her softly on the back. It was completely strange for him to be in a town where people knew anything real about him. Anything more than the media spin that his people worked so hard to produce.

Lee Ann pulled away and patted the part of the table across from Katie. "You sit now with our Katie, we'll get you two the special and some of Marv's fries."

It didn't seem like Roman had a choice. He slid into the booth, unzipping his coat and took off his beanie, completely mystified by this town.

Lee Ann frowned, studying him. "But you probably don't eat fried food, do ya?" She tapped her chin and then, without warning, reached out her hand to touch the stubble on his chin. Then she let out a yip laugh and yanked her hand back. "Oh, dear." A blush appeared on her face. "I'm sorry. I'm so sorry. It's just, you've always been my favorite, and I've been hoping all these years to finally meet you." She yip laughed again. She sucked in a breath and then patted her hair against the top of her forehead. "Oh, dear. What you young men and your charms can do to us older women."

Roman had no idea what to say. So he simply smiled. "Nice to meet you Lee Ann, thanks for all your support."

She sighed. "Ahh, maybe you get some time off being so strict with your diet because you guys just won the big game!" She put her hand up to give him a high five. "So do you want fries?"

He blinked and returned the high five. "Bring me Lizard fries."

Another yip laugh and she bustled away, before halfway turning back. "But I'm not even going to ask you if you want a soda 'cause you definitely don't need all that carbonation." She gave a stern nod and kept walking.

He watched her go and then turned to look at Katie.

The mischievous look on her face told him that she thought the whole exchange hilarious. She started to bust up. "Wolfe Creek Bachelor. I'm going to start filming."

The strange thing was that he'd come into this place completely ready to give this red-haired devil a piece of his mind. This girl who thought she could get him to buy all this stuff and then insist that she drive the snow mobile. And then, stalk off like she knew he would follow her. But he couldn't stop himself. He cracked up, too, and rubbed his cheek, feeling the red creep up his neck. "Was it weird she touched my face? 'Cause that felt weird."

Her green eyes sparkled, and she reached for her water. "Wow." She took a sip.

He took a sip of his water and grinned back at her. "What?"

Closing her eyes for a second, she kept her glass between her hands. "Is that what it's like for you all the time?"

He knew what she meant, but he didn't know how to respond. "I don't know."

"You don't know?" She leveled him with a serious look.

Uncomfortable, without really having a reason to be, he shrugged. "It's …" thoughts of his ex-wife and the other women that constantly threw themselves at him flooded his thoughts. The past few months it had gotten real old. He averted his eyes. "It's complicated."

She chug laughed, took a spoon, fished an ice cube out of her water and popped it into her mouth. "I'm sure," she said with her mouth full of ice cube.

He watched her try to bite on the too big piece of ice in her mouth and couldn't stop himself from grinning. "Is that a good piece of ice?"

For a second she paused, and then her cheeks flamed red. She took a piece of ice out of her glass and tossed it at him. "Be quiet." She finally crunched the ice, gulping back a laugh.

This naturally led him to act like a junior high kid, and he took a piece of ice out of his glass, tossing it back at her.

While crunching her ice and dodging the ice being thrown at her, she kept laughing. Then the laughing turned to choking.

He thought she was faking at first. Then he realized her eyes were slightly bulging and all the pounding she was doing on her chest wasn't a joke.

He panicked and stood, thinking of his training—like forever ago—on CPR, first aid, and the Heimlich. He jumped up and moved to her.

Coughing and coughing, her eyes were watering fiercely.

Tugging her out of the booth, he put his arms around her, hoping the ice wouldn't cut her throat or he wouldn't make her throw up. The problem with doing things like this was that he was strong. Not to mention adrenaline hyped at the moment. He latched his arms around her and squeezed.

She coughed, sputtered, and then put her hands up. "I'm okay. I'm okay."

Every part of him was keyed up. He released her and spun her around to see for himself.

The moment went slow and sticky and exactly what he remembered the first time he'd kissed his first girlfriend in the tenth grade after prom. His heart pounded at an unreasonable level, and without warning he was lost in her eyes.

Her cheeks were flushed and she was breathing heavily. It was totally silly for him to think about the fact she was much taller than his first kiss Becky Mueller had been in the tenth grade. She was shorter than his ex-wife by two or three inches. He focused on her slightly puffy lips. Then he noticed the blood on her lip.

Immediately, he reached for her lip and touched it with his thumb. "You're bleeding?"

She tried to back up, but only stumbled back into the booth.

He grabbed her shoulders. "Take a breath, it's okay."

After gulping in a breath, she steadied herself. "Sorry," she said, touching her lip, "I guess the whole face touching thing does feel 'weird.'"

Instantly, he dropped her shoulders, still fighting the crazy urge to kiss her. He took a step back and shook his head, covering his embarrassment with a grin. "Sorry, that was … are you okay?" He slid back into the booth.

She sat and then laughed. "I'm sorry. Gosh, how embarrassing."

He looked around. "I don't think anybody saw."

"No, I mean for you."

"Me?"

"Yeah, you touched my face." A wicked glint flashed into her eyes.

Roman realized she was teasing him. He grinned and leaned back into the booth. "Well, is it like that for you all the time?"

Without missing a beat, she dabbed a napkin to her lip. "Only when the fans get out of control."

Before either of them had a chance to say another word, Lee Ann reappeared. She was carrying two huge sandwiches, which Roman noticed were on some kind of homemade rye bread. The fries were piled so high that a couple fell off the plate as she put them down. "Whew." Lee Ann grinned at him and then winked. "Okay, Marv's famous chicken salad." She patted Katie softly on the shoulder. "You two enjoy. I'll get you some more water."

"Thank you." Katie patted her hand.

"Thanks," Roman said. He focused on the plate and decided Marv had talent. It smelled heavenly.

At first they both just ate and Roman had no idea what to say, but then Katie filled the silence by talking about her seven year old son, Josh, and his science project with twenty frogs living together in an aquarium. After they finished eating, they took the supplies back to the inn, and Katie good-naturedly bossed him around, telling him to take various supplies to different parts of the cabin. Some even went out to what she referred to as the 'barn,' which ended up being a huge shop behind the cabin.

Before he knew it, they were both pulling up the carpet on the stairs and hauling the pad and carpet to the barn. Katie showed him the process of getting the old furnace working. The furnace, along with the fireplace provided plenty of warmth. He took the cue that Katie was more focused on her work than doing anything else, so he tried to do the same—focus on the work, not look at Katie as much as he wanted to. Beneath the Carhartt suit she wore yoga pants and a worn Philadelphia Thunderbirds t-shirt. Of course he wasn't petty enough to make a crack about how awful that team was, but he definitely thought the shirt was a good deterrent from looking at her.

Finally, she asked, "So are you selling the place or what?"

He didn't answer immediately. "I'm not sure." Which was kind of true as of about two seconds ago.

She stood up and tugged back a lock of hair that had gotten loose from the ponytail she'd assembled before they started work in earnest. "You should reconsider because the Alaskan Inn means something here."

"What?" He tugged off the leather work gloves she'd insisted they buy for him earlier and picked up a bottle of water.

The way Katie Winters rolled her eyes and gave him a slight nostril flare made him want to laugh.

How rare it was to find a woman that treated him like ... a man. Just a man. Not a football player, not someone to be manipulated or worked over for some ad they wanted to run. He snorted.

She shook her head back and forth. "Your uncle made this place into a legacy. He made it something that families came back to every year. Did you know I've been getting calls from families that came to this place when they were kids? Now they have grandkids and want to bring them here."

Roman snorted again. "Seriously? This place is a dump." Before he'd even let the words come all the way out, he wanted to take them back.

Her lips pursed together and she glared at him, shaking her head. If she were a cartoon, smoke would be coming out her ears. "Do you even realize what it means to have a home?" she spat out. "Some place that means something."

He didn't respond. She looked like she was just getting started.

"Your uncle gave you this place because he loved it, and he obviously loved you. Now, you can either disregard something that's old because you think there's no life left in it, or you can work and mold it and give it a new life. That's your choice." She pointed at him then moved down the stairs. "But if I were you, I would hold on and thank God everyday that you have something to hold on to."

He watched her walk away and felt the adrenaline spiking through him. That woman made him want to rip something. So he continued to rip out carpet. Hearing her footsteps fading away, he muttered to himself, "There's nothing worth holding onto that doesn't hurt you."

Two hours later, the carpet was out, and they were starting to fix the subfloor.

Katie jerked to a standing position. "Oh my gosh! I have to go get Josh!" She dropped her hammer on the stairs and dashed for her winter gear.

Panic surged inside of him. Roman didn't know what to do with the silly lost puppy feeling that suddenly washed through him. He'd been with her all day, and as she dashed off, he suddenly came back to the present. The present where she was married to someone else with a kid. He stumbled down the stairs in his haste to catch her before she left. "When will you be back?"

Shoving on the pink pom, pom cap, she turned to face him and gave him a wink. "Don't look so desperate, quarterback, you're not getting rid of me that easy. Tomorrow. Same time, same place."

CHAPTER 3

THE REST OF THE AFTERNOON AND evening was filled with two impressive things. Roman finished getting all the pad and carpet out to the barn and he even pounded in or replaced nails. On two of the steps he had to tear off the tops and he went to the barn and found scraps to replace them. He brought them into the house to show Katie tomorrow morning and then cleaned up the workspace, feeling quite satisfied with himself.

A knock sounded at the kitchen door, and he quickly pushed through to find Mrs. K smiling through the glass windows. He flung the door back, making room for her to come in.

She didn't budge, staring him up and down. "She worked ya, did she?"

"She's a task master for sure." Worry flooded him about the cancer Katie had told him about.

Mrs. K grinned and handed over a warm container that looked to have soup and foil that contained some kind of hot bread. "You go get some rest, young man. I'll see ya in the morning."

Immediately, Roman rushed for his wallet on the table. "Here, let me pay you."

"Oh heavens," she was already trudging down the steps and headed for the small trail between their houses. "Your grandfather paid me well enough. I just thought there would be no one to look after you, so I thought I'd help out a bit."

Warmth swelled in Roman and he waved. "Thanks, Mrs. K."

She stopped and turned back. "Go up to the new room. I went ahead and made it up for you."

After scarfing down the soup and sumptuous bread, he couldn't shake the thought of Mrs. K struggling with cancer. Which was odd for him. He couldn't remember the last time he'd worried about someone else's health. He shook his head. He would have to find out more about that.

But what he needed right now was a good, long shower. He grabbed his bag as he headed up the stairs to find the guest room she spoke of. In the hallway, the animal heads assaulted him. Geese. Deer. Bear. Oh criminy—pigeon! He realized he remembered it all from his previous visits. He shook his head as he passed a horrific nineteen-seventies looking pigeon room with a rainbow Afghan on the wall.

He got to the end of the hall and hesitated. This was his uncle Jim's room. When Roman first spoke with the attorney, Mr. Burcher had told him he should clear out any personal effects of his uncle's that he wanted. Roman had responded that he didn't want any personal effects and the attorney had told him that a cleaning crew would remove it before the sale.

He peeked the door open and was surprised to see an ultra-bright-white down filled comforter on a king bed, with royal blue and white pillows all over. The curtains were open and Roman saw what looked to be, a newly painted and remolded master bathroom. The entire space was completely different from the other rooms. There were modern granite counters in the bathroom and a tiled shower that had sprayers coming from every which way.

A small note was propped up on the king-size bed. "Stay here."

He dropped his bag on the bed and ventured over to the sliding door that opened onto a gigantic deck. Roman pushed the door back and saw new planks of wood and steam coming up from a hot tub, surrounded by modern-looking deck furniture.

Without thinking much about it, he stripped down to nothing and immediately went to the hot tub. He vaguely remembered how this room should look, but he reckoned his uncle must have started the remodel on the inn a few months before his passing.

He tugged off the top and slid into the hot tub. It felt heavenly to his aching muscles. With the power outage, he would have expected the water to only be warm, but it was actually slightly too hot, just the way he liked it.

Snow still fell fast and furious, but the balcony was shielded by the roof that extended further than the deck. Roman watched the snow falling and first felt all the tension in his legs and back relax before he was finally able to let his shoulders relax. He loved hot tubs.

Cut off. He lay back against the hot tub and soaked in the fact that nobody was trying to call him, interview him, or bug him about how to handle his career. About his physical therapy. About keeping himself in the media enough to sell things, but not enough to get into trouble.

He grinned as he thought of Katie calling him quarterback. He recalled the way her voice had that teasing lilt to it and her eyes would narrow. He thought he might try to call her Kat, thinking he'd be funny—but instantly he knew that name wouldn't stick. No. He was sure she was Irish with that red hair. Katie was probably short for Katherine. He cocked his head to the side. His grandmother had been a Katherine. His mother's mom. He blinked. Not thinking about his grandmother, passing shortly after his mother passed. Not thinking about his mother. He wiped the back of his hand over his eyes. Definitely not thinking about Uncle Jim. He sucked in a breath and watched the snow fall. "Why didn't you tell me you were dying, ya old coot?"

CHAPTER 4

LOUD BANGING WOKE HIM UP THE NEXT morning, but it wasn't the happy sounds of pots rattling inside a kitchen while preparing breakfast. It was the bam, bam, bam of a hammer hitting nails. He tried to ignore it, turned on his side and covered the side of his head with a pillow. It didn't work.

When the pounding turned to sawing, he gave up completely. He threw back the covers, slid on a pair of jeans, and stumbled out of the room, knowing full well who it was. If he were the boss of this project, however benign this project was, he would refuse to let her start so early. For the love of all that was good and holy, he didn't often get a vacation like this where he wasn't at the demands of trainers waking him every dang morning.

He saw her on the steps immediately. Today she wore a red tank top with her red locks braided back, only slight wisps of hairs flowing out. Different yoga pants, not that he should be paying attention to that. He knew she meant serious business because she wore work boots, the kind that protect your toes. Before his anger could get the best of him, he was thrown off balance by the muscles in her arms.

She looked up and gave him a look. The kind of look that reminded him of a runner ready to go into a full sprint at any moment.

Another round of pounding started.

"Wait!" He held his hands up. "Stop that!"

Katie stayed in her pose. She had a female Thor kind of thing going. "Finally got up, lazy bones?"

His hands checked his pockets for his phone. Nothing. He scanned the hall. No clocks. "What time is it?"

With a half smile, Katie pounded another nail. "It's roughly seven-thirty." She gestured to the window, which still showed a thick blanket of snow coming down. "I figured you professional athletes would have to get up way early to get all your workouts done. Ya know, all those *important*, busy things you do."

Okay. Roman knew she'd kind of had a chip on her shoulder about football players since they'd met, but he hadn't realized it was this bad. He could not let her get away with this. "If excelling in a brutal sport so proficiently that you become one of the top players in America—even one of the top in the world—means you're lazy?" He held up his hands in surrender. "Then I guess you've caught me."

She glared at him for a second then went back to the banging. "If you don't want to hear banging, then go stay at another bed and breakfast because I was given direct instructions to rehab this place before we open for clients again this spring. That's t-minus sixty days, and every day I'm going to be pushing harder and harder."

Damn. Even though her attitude pissed him off, Katie was beautiful when she was angry. Flushed, eyes bright, every part of her tensed and engaged.

"Well?" She completely gave her attention to him and demanded an answer.

He didn't know what to say. So he settled for shaking his head. "I'm not paying you some crazy overtime morning rate, am I?"

At this, she rolled her eyes and went back to hammering. "You're paying me twenty bucks an hour for thirty hours a week." She pounded another nail. Her eyes flipped up at him. "Just so you know, your uncle always threw in a ten dollar lunch allowance, and he always counted my lunch as a working hour."

"I don't think so." He didn't really care. He just wanted to argue.

The next steps she took, flying up the steps, made him stumble back down the hallway to keep himself centered. She was in his face, shaking her finger. "Just so you know, while I'm so sorry to inconvenience the great Roman Young's football schedule, I am a single mother. I get up at five, run on my treadmill, do two loads of laundry, make lunch, clean up, make sure Josh's homework is done, get him off to school, and then I come here. I made sure," she was visibly trembling as she finally caught her breath before continuing, "that your uncle's bedroom was rehabbed before he died and you got here. That the hot tub was installed. That a down blanket was on the king *sleep number* bed. That top of the line jet sprayers were in that bathroom." Her face turned sad. "And then I would go visit him in that god forsaken care center in Ogden twice a week." She cocked an eyebrow. "Which I never let him pay me for." She shook her head. "Your uncle was a kind, good man. You should be grateful you had him. And...I'm trying to get this all done like he wanted."

He'd woken and sobered up. Fast. "Yes, he was." He suddenly felt sheepish. She'd done all that. All that for...him. His uncle had wanted that for him. Shame coursed through him. Shame and anger and pain that his uncle hadn't told him. But the thing that really stood out from this lecture was one fact. "You're not married?"

She held up her hand with the ring on it. "No, idiot, I'm married."

"Then why did you call yourself a single mom?" he shot back.

Her face paled, and she backed away, going down the steps.

He followed. "What?"

"It's a long, clichéd, boring story." Quickly, she tugged her winter gear into place and replaced her boots.

He was confused. The bulldog worker that had been terrorizing him suddenly wanted to leave. "What's going on?"

Her face was still pale. She pushed her pink pom pom hat into place and tugged one her boots and gloves. "I—I just have to go."

Suspicion stirred inside of him. "What happened to your husband?" An overwhelming urge to know assaulted him. He stepped in front of the side door so she couldn't leave. He didn't know why he sounded so fierce. Why thinking about her, wearing a ring and not living with her husband, made his venture into marriage and divorce seem real again.

She blinked a few times and then glared at him, defiance in her eyes. "None of your business."

All the angst and worry from his own marriage bubbled up. "He cheated on you?"

The look on her face went quickly from defiance to complete anger. She slapped him. Hard.

Then she covered her face and seemed dazed. "Don't EVER say that. I'm sorry. I'm sorry. I have to go." She pushed past him, almost completely getting stuck in the soft layer of snow by the stairs. But she recovered and moved to one of the snowmobiles.

It wasn't that Roman minded a good slap now and then. He didn't mind it if he deserved it. But he didn't think he had deserved it. He was on her side. Before he knew what he was doing, he had on his winter clothes and had grabbed the keys for the other snow mobile. He took off after her, centering his sunglasses on his face to prevent snow from getting in his eyes. The weather hadn't lightened up a bit.

He followed her and finally caught up when she slowed in front of a rocky field. When he was a little closer, he saw the lone stone-twisted metal arch that simply said Cemetery. He came to a stop behind her snowmobile. She'd pulled to the side of the cemetery and was trudging through the snow, some parts coming up to her hip.

Even though it was probably completely inappropriate, and even though he didn't know why he was doing it, he trudged after her.

She looked up when he was two steps away, as if she hadn't heard him park. "Why are you here?"

He frowned and looked at the grave she'd cleaned off. "I don't know."

Her breaths were loud, and then they gradually evened out. They both just stood there. The snow fell in waves around them, making him feel like they were almost the last two people on earth. "What happened?"

She didn't answer for a couple of minutes, but he waited. "Another cliché story—car accident." She shrugged, and tears fell down her cheeks. "He'll be gone a year tomorrow." She looked hollow and sad and tired.

Roman wanted to reach out to her, pull her into him, shield her from this pain. But, of course, he didn't. That would be insane. He hardly knew her. "A local boy?"

She closed her eyes for a second and then flipped them open. "How come you make it sound so...so...trite?"

"I didn't mean it that way." And he hadn't. "I'm sorry. I just wondered if you grew up together." Honestly, he didn't know what to say. All he knew was that he felt like if he quit talking, it would be worse.

"Yes, we grew up here. We used to own the farm on the way into town. It was sold three months after he died." She shrugged. "I couldn't keep up the payments."

It was all slipping into place. "So that's why you know how to fix everything?"

She nodded and bit into the side of her lip. "Your uncle came to me at Josh's funeral and asked me to take over his place. He was still living there, but he'd quit taking guests. Mrs. K just cooked for him. He could still get around okay, and you know he didn't need the money from the business. At the time I told him I couldn't do it, but all he did was hand me a key and tell me that the Lord would provide. Then a check started showing up every month for 30 hours a week at 20 dollars an hour."

A slow tear leaked out, and she swiped at it angrily. "You know, that's how small towns are. They fill needs where they can. And your uncle was one of those people who just helped people, with nothing in it for himself."

Out of nowhere, Roman felt his own tears threaten and then spill. His uncle always spoke about how the scriptures said your left hand should not know what the right hand was doing. He was selfless. He served, not to gain a spot in the media, but to be the best man he could be.

A stab of remorse fell through Roman. He wanted to be that man. He wanted to be a man that someone cried over when he was dead. Really cried and not because they wouldn't win at football. No. He wanted to do something real. Something that changed people's lives.

"So after I lost the farm, I used my savings to rent a small house in town. I took the key for the place and got to work. He'd been put in the care center in Ogden by this time, but he'd left the list of what he wanted done. I would go chat with him about how it was turning out. I took pictures to show him. Obviously, the list just kept growing." She shrugged and grinned at him. "I like to make new lists."

He hesitated, roughly wiping his face. "I noticed."

Her face lit up. "Did you use the hot tub?" She truly looked hopeful and happy that he would be pleased with it.

He couldn't help grinning. "It was the perfect touch."

"And you liked the sleep number bed? I got that at a super great sale."

Touching his lower back, he marveled, "Back doesn't hurt at all."

Keeping her smile in place, she nodded. "Well, I'm glad to hear it."

Roman let out a sigh, trying to absorb all this new information. "So it's a good thing I didn't show up when it was a real dump earlier?"

"Exactly." She laughed. She looked around and then back at him. "So now you know more than you ever wanted to know about Katie Winters. I'm a Wolfe Creek resident. Single mom. Widow."

He shook his finger at her. "You mean the great Katie Winters."

Wistfully, she lifted an eyebrow. "I don't know about that."

Something shifted inside of him as he studied the vulnerability in her eyes. Something he couldn't quite put a finger on. Perplexed, he tried to clear his mind and think of something to say. "I don't know, Katie Winters, I think I might want to know more."

Their eyes held, locked for a few seconds, then she shifted back to the gravestone.

Gingerly, he stepped forward and read, "Joshua Winters, beloved husband and father."

Katie touched the top of it. "I know beloved is cliché, but it's true."

Inexplicable pain surged through Roman. He wanted to take away all of Katie's heartache, this thing that obviously kept her running, driven to keep the bills paid. His eyes were suddenly opened to her problems. Actual problems—not just how many grams of protein she took in a day.

He stared at the grave and then bent to trace the initials. "I don't think beloved is cliché at all. I called my mother beloved." His voice was quiet.

"Oh." Her voice was soft, and she turned to look at him. "You did?"

He nodded. "It wasn't fast…it was long. Four years. Lots of treatments. She was the best mom a boy could have."

"Your father?" She asked.

He scoffed, "Left when I was two. Didn't look back. I couldn't care less about him. The only man I truly cared for, and who cared for me, was Jim." More sadness pressed on his chest and moisture filled his eyes. "He paid for my mother's medical expenses." He wiped his eyes. "He loved me before I was a star, after I lost myself in my career, and even when I wasn't sure who I was." He closed his eyes.

Without warning, Katie took his gloved hand in hers and moved him down the rows of markers. She pointed. His uncle's looked fresh, new. The message on it was 'To all the people in this town—it's been a fun ride. To R...I love you. Go Destroyers!'

A laugh jerked out of him before he could get a hold of his mixed emotions. He shook his head. "They were always his favorite team." A river of tears traced down his cheeks and then anger bubbled. He clenched his fist. "Why didn't he call me? Why did he tell that attorney NOT to call me for the funeral?"

It was silent, and then Katie answered. "I didn't realize he had told the attorney not to call you. I just...it doesn't matter what I thought." She hesitated. "But you know how he was. He knew you had playoffs and the championship game. He knew you'd worked so hard to get your knee back in shape, and he knew you might get a shot. I'm sure he didn't want to tell you and have you blow it."

More tears spilled down his cheeks.

This time, her naked hand reached for his face and gently brushed away the tears.

Before he knew what he was doing, he slipped his own glove off and took her hand.

What happened next could only be called a mixing of time and breath and a little bit of magic. As Roman stared in her eyes, he knew what he felt for Katie Winters was something he'd never felt for anyone else in his entire life.

CHAPTER 5

HE COULDN'T HAVE EVEN GUESSED HOW long they'd both stood there, holding hands, staring into each other's eyes. All he knew was that it was too soon when Katie carefully took back her hand and turned for the snowmobile. "I have to get back to work."

It might be too soon for him to expect her to acknowledge what had just happened between them. In fact, if truth be told, he had no idea what had just happened, but c'mon, something had. He caught up to her and tried not to feel like a teenager. "Why don't we go get breakfast?"

She slipped onto the snowmobile, all business. "I have things that need to get done today." She started the engine.

This abrupt attitude was more than he could handle. He reached across her and shut off the snowmobile. "I'm your boss, and I say what gets done today." There. See? He could be bossy, too.

Titling her chin up, she gave him her signature defiant look. A somewhat sexydefiant look, but he wasn't noticing that he told himself. Yes, it mattered that she wasn't...attached...but for heaven's sake, now wasn't the time to start something. Guilt tugged inside of him for even thinking about it. He wouldn't even be here longer than it took for the roads to clear and Mr. Burcher to get back here to do paperwork with him.

Pinching her lips together, she shrugged. "Fine."

Her resignation was not what he expected. "What?"

"Command me, oh bossiness."

He rolled his eyes. "I am not the bossy one! Pshaa, no way. Did you see yourself bossing me here and there yesterday?"

She threw her hands into the air, totally exasperated. "Quit talking, QB, and get on the snowmobile." She gestured behind her. "We'll come back for the other one later."

Waiting a beat, he stared at her, confused that he could feel this mixture of anger and attraction to her.

After starting the snowmobile, she grinned at him. "I guess you can just buy breakfast instead of lunch."

When he finally complied and got on behind her, she took off, taking their speed up fast.

This forced him to hold her tighter, and he could help inhaling her light lemony smell.

She laughed as she brought their speed down and turned onto Main Street.

The snow was still coming down in a blanket. But it had calmed down a bit. He couldn't imagine that the weather would clear enough to get the plows through. Secretly, he didn't mind spending another day with Katie.

They passed the hardware store, and he thought she would pull into the Leaping Lizard, but she took a sharp right turn and kicked up their speed a notch as she headed toward what looked to be a huge ski resort.

Roman studied the monstrous development that he hadn't realized was nestled at the base of this mountain. Granted, there weren't that many cars in the giant parking lot, but he was sure there would be during the peak ski times. He'd never been a skier. Never lived in a place that afforded that opportunity and never really cared to take it up. His ex-wife had told him it would be good for his image, but he'd never understood why it would matter. She'd said it would make him look daring.

He wondered if Katie would take them to the resort. There looked to be a lot of shops and places to eat. Some appeared open and others looked empty, but she took a turn away from the resort side and went up a small road, a road that had an old sign hanging on a large tree over the road.

The Wolfe's Haven.

She parked in front of a somewhat older looking home that had a bunch of snowmobiles in front of it, and the smell of coffee filled the air.

Roman's stomach rumbled. As they walked up, he took note of the quaint wrap around deck that had tables covered in snow and chairs stacked on top of each other in rows.

The door chimed as they walked in. The place had the feel of an old mom and pop shop, with a soda fountain bar and back splash mirror. The whole place was faded reds and blacks with large posters of Elvis and Marilyn Monroe, James Dean and some others he didn't recognize, but knew his mother would have recognized them. Country music played out of the juke box to the side of the door and Roman stared at the men sitting at the counter talking and holding newspapers. He imagined that the coffee never ran out here.

Katie smiled and said hello to some people. She stopped when a man with a kitchen towel wrapped around his waist appeared from behind the revolving door and came out with his hands full of plates. "Lou, this is Jim's nephew."

The man paused for a second. Roman surmised that he was probably around his own age—late twenties. Roman measured him the way he would any player on the field. The man was fit, six footish. Probably played ball in high school. He would be fast. He looked Italian and had a mustache and brown eyes. He glared at Roman for a second then nodded. "Be right with you guys."

Katie led them through the restaurant that opened up to a huge glass window on the other side that faced up the mountain. He could see one of the lifts right next to the building, with an operator helping skiers go up.

Katie took a seat next to the window and Roman sat across from her.

He was captivated by the snow. By the way the town kept going even though it felt like nothing should be going. In Texas, this kind of snow would cripple them.

Katie shrugged off her Carhartt. Her lean limbs were revealed in her tank top and yoga pants. She tugged a blue scarf out of her pocket and wrapped it around her neck and smoothed back her hair. Even though it seemed funny to Roman that she would do that, he jerked open his menu

"Hmm." Katie opened her menu. "The waffles are the best here, and they'll even sub them for pancakes when you get an omelet."

Roman pretended to read the menu, slightly annoyed at himself that he felt a twinge of jealousy at the way Lou had looked at her.

She flipped the pages. "This restaurant has been in Lou's family for generations. This land is actually owned by his family. They just lease it to the ski resort. That was back when resorts would do that kind of thing—share with families. Now most of them just want to own the land and open their own corporate things."

Trying not to dwell on how much she was talking about Lou, he decided on a ham and cheese omelet with waffles. His nutritionist could ream him later. "That's nice."

A server came and introduced herself. "Well, hello there." She stopped as she studied Roman. "Can I just say that television makes you look exactly as good as I'd always pictured you would?"

Roman could feel the red creeping up his cheeks. He blinked. "Well, you look good, too." It came out woodenly, but, Roman realized the girl with the nametag that said 'Tiffany'—who was blond and probably in her early twenties with a lean figure—did look good.

At his compliment, Tiffany's grin widened. She lightly smacked Roman's shoulder. "Heaven's, Roman Young, you do know how to give a girl a compliment."

He grinned back at her, suddenly feeling comfortable.

"Hmm." Katie cleared her throat. "I'm at the table too, Tiffany."

Immediately, Tiffany jerked her gaze away from Roman. A frown touched her lips. "Katie Winters, how come I'm not surprised that you're sitting here—with the man I claimed a long time ago." She cocked a hand on her hip. "A long, long time ago." She shook her finger at Katie. "His uncle used to come in here and tell me all about Roman, and I told his uncle that if he ever came to town, he had to hook me up. I've been the first in line since the divorce."

If Roman could have known this would happen, he definitely would have avoided coming here and this little soap opera he'd just been made some kind of star in.

Katie pinched her lips and narrowed her eyes. "I'm. Not. Interested. In Roman."

The words ricocheted inside Roman's head.

Tiffany eased a smile back into place and put a pen to a pad of paper. "Good." She gave her a meaningful look, and Roman knew that whatever small town rivalry had gone on between them would probably be an interesting story. "Well," Tiffany said, recovering, "now that all the unpleasantness is out of the way, what will you have for breakfast?"

***

They'd spent the next few minutes ignoring Tiffany's little outburst. Katie seemed bugged and Roman didn't know what to say.

Roman watched people get on the lift. Most of them looked like locals or seasoned skiers. He could tell this by the wear and tear of their equipment. It felt like he could spot a newbie a mile away. He let out a sigh, unable to keep up with the silence. "I guess getting trapped at a ski resort for a couple of days could only improve skiing for people, right?"

Katie pretended that she didn't hear him. Or, if she had, she didn't acknowledge him.

If there was anything that Roman didn't like, it was being ignored. "Look, if you'd rather not talk to me because you fear angering your high school nemesis, then that's fine—say that. But don't just ignore me. It's rude."

Her eyes flashed anger as she flicked her head, and their eyes met. The emotion made her eyes an intense green. The kind of green that looked almost blue. Ocean green. The kind he'd seen on several trips to Hawaii when he'd gone snorkeling and scuba diving with Sheena. At the memory, he yanked his gaze away.

She still didn't say anything.

He turned back to her. "And, by the way, I don't appreciate you announcing to the whole town that I'm Jim's nephew everywhere we go." He didn't turn to look at her. It *did* bother him that she felt like she had to tell everyone, to explain the only reason she would be seen with him or something.

"But you are Jim's nephew." Her voice was low.

His leg bounced with nervous energy. He put his hand on it to stop it. "Well, they'll find out soon enough, you don't need to tell everyone like…like that's the only reason you're with me…because you're stuck with me." It was exactly how he felt, but it sounded ridiculous, the vulnerability tripping out of his lips.

For a second she didn't say anything. Then she let out a dramatic sigh. "You don't think this whole town will immediately recognize you? Wait, they might be confused you're not with your wife. Sara, Sheila—?

"Sheena," he finished for her.

She turned to face him. "You mean the super model." Sarcasm washed over her face.

She was jealous? He frowned. "Look, you don't need to compare yourself to her."

From the look on her face, he could tell the words meant that he'd meant to soothe her, had only served to tick her off. She leaned forward. "Don't flatter yourself, QB. There's only one thing you can bet on in a small town, that people talk. And, well, I have had enough of being talked about for a long, long time. And my son doesn't need that, either. So, yes, I'm up front and honest with people about stuff because I figure they'll find out anyway. I may as well be truthful."

The way her fierce pride filled every word made him grin.

She faltered. "Why are you smiling?"

He didn't want to admit that he found her pride and fierceness attractive, so he asked about her son. "How did Josh's report go for science yesterday?"

Obviously, she hadn't been expecting this turn in conversation. "Fine," she answered quickly.

"Good." He turned as Tiffany came back to the table and put down their drinks. She winked at Roman before moving away. "Your food will be out in a sec."

He took a sip of water and kept his face innocent, even though he felt guilty for some reason.

Katie relaxed, leaning back. The side of her lip turned up. "The frogs somehow jumped out and took off down the hall. It took them twenty minutes to round them all up."

Roman let out a laugh. "No."

A grin spread across her lips, and all Roman could think about was how pretty she was. She reached for her glass. "His poor teacher sent a note home for me that asked to please not send science projects to school that could jump."

More laughter came out of Roman, and he envisioned a bunch of second graders chasing twenty frogs around the school. Thinking of the chaos that would have ensued brought on more laughter.

Shaking her head, she grinned. "Ahh, teachers should be sainted." She took her spoon and scooped out a piece of ice.

His hand shot out and intercepted the ice. "Can you be trusted not to kill yourself today?"

Leveling him with a glare, she wrinkled her nose and took the ice off her spoon, popping it into her mouth. "Poor Mr. Hansen, he's a good teacher."

Happy for neutral ground, Roman nodded. "Sounds like it."

They both held each other's eyes and Roman could have sworn that Katie blushed. Feeling a rush of heat on his own face, he turned away.

Tiffany came with their food, piling the table with the extra plates of waffles. She went to a side table and got a pitcher of water, filling up the glasses. She focused on Roman. "Is there anything else I can get for you?"

He nodded to Katie. "Katie, is there anything else you need?"

Katie met his gaze and then gave a mock smile to Tiffany. "No."

Tiffany returned the mock grin and then put a light hand on Roman. "So, have you had anyone show you the sights since you've been here? I know it's been snowy, but the view from the top of this mountain is breathtaking. If you haven't been, I could show you after work?"

Uncomfortable, but not taken off guard, Roman let out a sigh. "Darn, I wish I could," he said, lifting a fork to point at Katie, "but Katie has me busy for the next couple of days."

Tiffany gave Katie an accusing glare.

Katie took the cue from Roman. "We're finishing a few things around the inn, but maybe you kids could play next week."

Tiffany held her stare and then shrugged and turned away. "I'll be back in a little bit."

Digging into his food, Roman let out a heavenly sigh. "You were right. These waffles are pretty good."

Katie took a bite of waffle and flashed a smile. "I told you."

When they were done, Roman sipped his water and looked out the window. He imagined the view from the top of the mountain was glorious.

"You want to know what the deal is with Tiffany, don't you?"

The fact that she'd brought it up told him that she wanted to talk about it. "Nope."

"It's awkward, right?"

"No."

"You said no too fast," she accused.

"I did?"

"You did."

"O-kay."

Her eyes twinkled. "If you don't want people to know you're lying, you have to pretend you're thinking about it. You didn't think about it."

"Wow, look at you, studying lying."

"I do have a communications degree."

"You do?

She grinned. "A master's degree. My thesis was on lying in relationships, courting relationships."

Suddenly he felt nervous. "Really?"

She smacked his hand and laughed. "But we're not courting, so you don't have to worry, I don't even think of you that way. You're my boss, right?"

"Right," he answered quickly. Then he tried to appear to be thinking about it. "I mean, of course, that's why we're here, cause you have one meal a day included."

She nodded. "You're just the new signer of the paychecks."

"Oh right." The food felt hard in his gut. "Yeah." He wondered if he answered too fast.

"So, that reminds me." She put her fork down. "I was thinking, that you could take out ad space for the inn with the ski resort and the boat rental place down at the marina by the lake."

The lake. Memories surged through him. He remembered going out on a boat with his uncle. "The lake."

Her eyes twinkled. "Yeah, the lake."

He shook his head. "I'd forgotten about the lake. Uncle Jim took me out on his boat when I was here." He grinned, thinking about feeling the water spray on his face and the sunburn he'd had the next day. But the best part had been seeing his mother water ski. Seeing her so alive and happy. They'd eaten ham and cheese sandwiches for lunch, and he remembered Uncle Jim burying him in the sand. "That was one of the best days of my life."

She cleared her throat.

He looked at her and caught her studying him. He blinked. "What?"

She blinked back. "Nothing. I mean, you—you look so sad sometimes."

He decided to be honest with her. "Uncle Jim gave me everything, and I gave him nothing. I-I guess being here reminds me of what a jerk I've turned into."

The moment seemed to slow, and she reached across the table and took his hand. "Your uncle loved you."

The pain that he'd been trying to push away came rushing at him full force, like a natural geyser in Yellowstone that burst with hot air. Tears pushed themselves out of his eyes. "No, I—" He didn't know why he was telling her this, but it all came tumbling out. "I was a fool. Sheena had this image she wanted to protect, and I see now that I got so caught up in that that I didn't realize all the important things that she took me away from."

Her eyes were so sympathetic. "I'm sorry." She kept her hand on his.

"I got hurt a few months ago and that, combined with—"

"With finding out your wife cheated on you." Her face had gone stone cold hard.

He was surprised. "You read the tabloids?"

She shook her head. "Your uncle told me you called him."

Hope sprung out of him. "He did?"

She smiled. "He was really happy to have you back in his life."

More tears spilled down his cheeks. "Then why didn't he tell me he was dying?"

She gently squeezed his hand. "I don't know, but like I told you before, I bet it was because he wanted you to get back on that field. He didn't want to mess that up for you."

A turmoil of emotion swirled through him. His uncle had always protected him. Helped him. Even still protected him when he needed Roman. He clenched a fist and put his head down, letting more tears come. "I can't be here."

"Roman." She held onto his hand.

He looked up.

Her eyes were bright, and a tear fell down her cheek. "This is exactly where you should be, don't you see that? Jim wanted you to come."

Guilt surged within him.

She swallowed and nodded. "It's okay. You're okay."

When she said those words a strange thing happened, the certainty she felt seared into him. She was right. He was okay. He took in a breath. "You're right."

Taking her hand back, she nodded. "It's okay."

They both sat, saying nothing.

Then she smiled. "So you'll look into that?"

"What?"

"The ad space."

He hated lying to her, but he didn't know how to tell her the truth. He looked out the window. "Sure."

"Why aren't you looking at me?"

He turned back. "I am looking at you."

"You're not going to look into it." She sighed and got out her phone.

"What are you doing?"

"I'm adding it to my list."

"No," he protested. "I'll do it."

"You will?" Her voice was doubtful.

He didn't know why, but he knew that if he told her he would, then he really would do it. "I will."

"Fine."

Letting out an exasperated sigh, she sipped the last of her water. "You would think that you weren't the owner."

LAST PLAY ◆ 73

"Stop. Okay. I...you've just been going at this since I met you. Man, you should have been a coach, you're relentless."

"Relentless?" She looked pleased at this description of her.

"Yes."

She threw her hands up. "I'm just trying to let you be the boss."

Oh no. This sounded way too emasculating for him. The quarterback of the Dallas Destroyers didn't need her permission for anything. "*Let* me be the boss?" he grinned.

She laughed. "Does that hurt your ego, QB?"

Reluctantly, he admitted to himself that he liked the way she said 'QB.' "No, it doesn't hurt my ego."

"Does, too." She pointed at him.

He swiped her finger away with his fork. "Does not."

They both grinned at each other.

He put his fork down. "Fine, if I'm the boss, then I say we take a day off and go sledding today."

"You do?"

"I've always lived in Texas, and one year we came to visit Uncle Jim for Christmas, and we...went sledding. It was the most fun thing I've ever done."

She scoffed, "You want to work on sledding?" She did not look amused.

He drizzled syrup on the fork, reasoning that if he weren't 'courting' Katie, it wouldn't matter if he sucked down syrup like a teenager, right? It felt good not to worry about how many carbs were in the syrup. He grinned. "I want to work on sledding."

She shook her head. "Fine, QB, we'll go sledding."

But before he could pay Tiffany and get out of there, Lou, the man from earlier, walked up to their table. He patted Katie on the back. "How are you?" His hand moved to her shoulder.

She smiled and covered his hand with hers. "Hey, I'm good." Her face became gentler when looking at Lou.

Unexpectedly, Roman tensed.

Lou turned to Roman, giving him an up and down. "So Roman Young returns to claim what's his."

The way Lou kept his hand on Katie's shoulder, felt like he was letting Roman know that he might be claiming the Inn, but he couldn't claim her, too. Roman gave him an easy smile. "Yep, just here checking out the place and helping Katie get a few things done."

Lou turned to Katie, keeping her hand in his. "My dear, why didn't you tell me you needed help?"

If Roman hadn't known better, he would think that Katie was actually blushing. "Oh no, it's fine. Roman offered, and since he's stuck here for a while...." She gestured to the snow falling. "I accepted his help."

"Hmph." Roman hadn't meant to contradict Katie. But really? Offered to help? He thought of having the list shoved at him and being told it was about time he got here.

Lou spun back to him, giving him the same sizing up that Roman had given Lou earlier. "Did you have something to say, Jim's nephew?" He glared at him again. "I thought it was a good call to go with Dumont in the big game. He did an excellent job."

The muscles in Roman's jaw flexed and adrenaline shot through him. One thing a quarterback easily recognizes when he looks at a man is when that man wants to hit him. He sees that look on the field all day, almost every day. Every part of Roman became very still, just like when he was about to throw the best touchdown of the game. Instantly, he knew. He knew Lou, indeed, had planned to mark his territory with Katie Winters. Roman put on his best media boy smile and laughed. "You're right. He did win it for us." he conceded.

Touching the side of his mustache with his other hand, Lou swallowed. "I guess I would be more on team Roman if you'd had the decency to show up to your uncle's funeral."

The floor scraped as Roman shoved out of the booth and the table shifted on the cement floor. He was tired of everyone assuming that he'd had a choice in the matter.

"Roman!"

He and Lou were now facing each other. Both of them had their fists clenched. Roman knew his agent would not be happy when this story broke—Destroyer's Quarterback takes out small town waiter.

"Roman!"

He swerved to face her, pulling back on his temper. "What?"

She pushed out of the booth and moved in between him and Lou. Her face was desperate. "Don't you remember you were going to take me sledding?"

Roman teetered between giving in to his temper and being better than that. Finally, he pulled his wallet out and dropped a hundred dollar bill on the table. He turned and shoved past Lou. "Then I guess we'd better go."

CHAPTER 6

THE HILL SHE TOOK HIM TO WAS...BIG. In Texas it would be considered a mountain. Here, it was considered a hill. Neither of them had talked about what had happened.

Katie had quickly gone to Jim's front closet and outfitted them both with better gear for sledding. She'd tried to crack some jokes, but he'd simply given tight smiles. He knew why Lou's comments ticked him off so much...because they were the truth.

They parked at the top, and then she handed him the tube. "You go first."

He didn't move. "Why did you do that?"

"What?"

"Back there with Lou."

Her face went serious. He couldn't help noticing that, even though her hair looked all fuzzy from the hat, her skin was flawless and a few freckles dotted her nose. He could honestly say she was one of the most naturally beautiful women he'd ever met. "I didn't think it was worth it."

He sucked in a breath. "You mean me blowing my top?" The media coverage had shown some not so nice scenes of him after the accident—drunk and frightened, which had translated into a fist into the side of his Ferrari. The dent mark had been all over the news.

"No." Her voice was clipped and she stuck her chin up. "I don't think it's worth it to defend something you know the truth about."

He frowned.

She pointed at him. "You know that you would have come if you'd have know." She gently tapped his chest. "You know. It doesn't matter what I thought, what everyone else thinks because *you* know the truth."

Chills washed over him. Her certainty filled him with a measure of hope. Pride. Something that he hadn't felt about himself in a long time. He liked it. He blinked and looked around. He didn't remember sledding on such a big hill. Nervous jitters wound through him. "That's a long way down."

She cocked an eyebrow. "Come here, would you mind if I took your picture for my son?"

He could tell that she didn't like asking for things. This made him want to give it to her. "Only if you're in it with me."

She hesitated.

He motioned her over to him. "C'mon, bachelorette, pretend like you want a rose tonight."

This made her laugh. They posed, and she snapped a picture.

"Thanks."

He liked being able to do something for her, even if it was just taking a picture. "You're welcome."

She gestured down the mountain. "Now, are you going to be a pansy, or are you going to take the hill like a man?"

Giving her a bored look, he ripped the tube away from her and threw it on the ground. He grunted and pounded his chest. He let out a war cry and jumped on the tube. "Me. Man!" he shouted.

Then he was flying. His speed picked up, and mists of snow flew around him. He could hear traces of her laughter behind him.

When he got to the bottom, she was whooping and hollering. "Oh yeah! That's what I'm talking about, that was awesome!"

He would be lying if he didn't feel satisfaction from her praise. He knew she meant it. She wasn't one of those baller girls hanging on his every word, trying to be something he wanted her to be so she could spend all his money and then cheat on him with his best friend. He grinned and gave another war cry back at her.

She clapped and laughed.

He stood still, watching her with her pink pom pom hat and her red hair coming in waves down her shoulders. Then he did something he never should have done. He wondered how it would feel to have her at the games, to look up and see her smiling and cheering him on.

He huffed back up to the top of the mountain, realizing that it wouldn't matter how many carbs he ate today. This trudging through deep snow would burn up everything.

When he got to the top, she had her arms crossed, an eyebrow lifted.

"What?" he asked, sucking in air and handing her the tube.

Her eyes narrowed. "Do you still love her?"

This question, he had not expected. For some reason it made him feel weird to have her ask it—like he couldn't lie to her but he couldn't tell her the truth. He purposely tried to think about it. "No."

She cocked her head to the side. "You can't try to pause. Then I know you're lying."

He threw his hands up. "I'm your boss. You're an employee. Why do you care if I love her?"

She looked him up and down. Then she shrugged. "You're right. I don't." She grinned. "Is sledding still as fun as you remember?"

He grinned. "The best."

"Worth paying me twenty bucks an hour? Because I'm collecting, QB."

He shook his head. "Worth every penny."

She put the tube down. "Want to go together?"

Confusion clouded his mind. "Why?"

An innocent grin filled her face. "Why not?"

Sitting down in the middle of the tube he patted his lap. "Hop on boss!"

"Wait." She motioned for him to stand. "Go on your stomach. I'll back up and give us a push as I jump on."

He acquiesced, thinking it was kind of close quarters. He flopped down, and before he knew what happened, she was pushing his feet to the edge of the hill and then hopping on top of him.

Granted, she didn't weigh much, and he didn't mind absorbing her weight. What he hadn't anticipated was how the extra weight would speed them up.

She let out a yell next to him. "Wahoo!"

His heart leapt in his chest, and he echoed her, "Whoo-hoo!"

Snow flew in their faces, but he glanced up at her. Her hair had gotten free—red curls flew in his face with the snow. He could honestly say that this was the first time in as long as he could remember that he felt like a kid.

They got to the bottom, and she quickly rolled off, laughing. "Oh my gosh, that was fun!"

He brushed himself up. "That *was* fun."

She got to her feet and grinned.

"Thanks for asking me." He meant it.

A wicked glint came into her eyes, and she backed up starting into a sprint up the hill. "You're carrying the tube, right? Come on, QB. I'll race ya to the top."

Now he understood. He watched her sprinting. She'd asked him because she wanted him to be the pack mule. But he had never been one to back away from a challenge. He grabbed the tube and took off. It wasn't hard to pass her. As he did, he turned around and taunted her, "C'mon, boss, never stop. Never quit."

She only grinned wider and winked at him. "Really, you're proud of yourself for beating a girl? That's pathetic."

At that, he laughed. This woman, she was driving him mad. This time, before she knew what was happening, he threw the tube down and grabbed her, holding on while he dove sideways onto the tube. "I'll show you pathetic."

A squeal louder than a foghorn came out of her. "Let me go!" She giggled.

Then they were off, flying down the hill. When they got to the bottom, he gently rolled off the tube and messed with her hair. "That's right, boss! I'm proud to beat a girl!"

More giggles erupted from her. At this moment she looked...so young. Child-like. He liked it.

"Stop!" she shouted.

He stopped, collapsing into a heap next to her by the tube.

She panted hard and turned onto her side to face him. "Dang, you're in good shape. What do you do—like running drills all day at work?"

He picked up a little piece of snow and tossed it in her hair. "No, apparently, I run an inn."

Trying to pick the snow he threw out of her hair, she flipped her hair back. "What about the injury? Are you going to go back out there?"

"If by going back out there, you mean am I going to keep playing football, the answer is yes." The conversation had taken on a serious tone. Granted, the media couldn't stop talking about which quarterback should have the shot. "If they give me a shot, I'll take it."

"Hmm." She eyed him top to bottom.

"Hmm," he mimicked, moving closer to her and wiping at a clump of snow in her hair.

Giggles erupted out of her for the second time. "What? Do I have snow in my hair?" She shook her hair at him.

It didn't matter what anyone said to him after this point. Right now, he knew he had to be with this woman. Suddenly he quit grinning, concerned by this realization.

Seeing him turn serious, she stopped giggling, too. "What's wrong?"

The hammering inside his chest reminded him of the first time he'd thrown the winning touchdown in the first championship game he'd won. "Nothing," he said too fast.

Squinting at him, she grinned. She stood. "C'mon, QB, don't be lazy. We can do a few more runs before I have to pick up Josh!"

CHAPTER 7

ROMAN HAD INSISTED ON GOING WITH her after they'd dropped the tube back at the inn, saying that he wanted to meet Josh. He'd followed her on a different snow mobile through Main Street, passed the hardware store and down the opposite direction from the ski resort. The road led to a small elementary school and a combined junior high and high school.

The snow had subsided substantially. Roman wondered how long it would be before the attorney would be able to get up to the inn to get the paperwork done to sell the place. He was surprised he actually didn't want to think about it. He pushed the thought away because it made him sad.

They waited with other snowmobiles or pretty hefty four-wheel drive vehicles for the kids to get out. They didn't have to wait long before a mass of children burst out of the building. He watched Katie wave to a child with a batman backpack and batman hat and gloves.

The boy came running quickly for the snowmobile. Roman noted that he had the shape of his mother's face and nose, but his hair was blonde. "Mom!" He held up some piece of paper. "Look, I painted this for you today!"

First, Katie hugged him. Then she kept her arm around him and studied the picture with a serious face. "I love it!"

Pure joy lit up the boy's face.

Katie nodded toward him and then tugged him by the hand. "I want you to meet someone."

Nervous seemed like an understatement for how Roman felt. Butterflies pounded into his gut. Meeting the most important man in any woman's life was a huge deal and he suddenly wondered if he was really ready for this.

Katie gestured to Roman. "Josh, meet Roman. This is Jim's nephew. He owns the inn now. He's been...helping me for the past two days."

Josh scrunched up his face, like meeting Roman was some sort of scientific project. "You look like that football player."

Roman put his hand out. "Roman Young, nice to meet you."

Tentatively, Josh put his batman glove in Roman's hand. "Could I get you to sign something?"

"Josh!" Katie shook her head.

Roman grinned. Young fans were the best. "Absolutely!" He released Josh's hand.

After fist pumping the air, Josh laughed. A loud, kid kind of laugh. "Now I can say I've met someone famous."

Katie gestured to the other snowmobile looking flustered. "Josh, it doesn't matter if someone is famous or not, every person is important. Please say goodbye, and let's go home and get you warmed up."

The boy didn't move, still studying Roman. "You play for the Destroyers, but you got hurt last year. Jim told me all about you."

The center of Roman's chest tightened for a second. He grinned. "Well, see, your mom told me all about your frogs getting out yesterday, so I guess we both know stuff about each other."

The boy gave a silly laugh and pointed at Roman. "I watched you play on that big screen at the inn last year."

Another surge of impossible emotion. "Well, thanks for watching."

Katie was already on the snowmobile. "Come on, son. Let's go."

Josh frowned. "Mom, can we have him over for dinner?"

This took Roman completely by surprise. "Hmm, no, I couldn't."

Katie looked stressed. "Josh, he probably has plans tonight. Let's do it another time."

Josh smiled at him. "Do you have plans?"

Roman looked from Josh to Katie.

She shrugged.

He grinned. "I'll be there."

CHAPTER 8

"NED, WHAT DO YOU MEAN, you won't be here for another two days?" Roman ran his hand through his hair. His agent was going to have a fit.

"Roman, I'm sorry. I put my back out, and I can barely move. I'm staying at my brother's house in Salt Lake. I was adjusted yesterday, but it might take a steroid shot to get my L4 back under control."

Flutters went through the pit of his stomach, and he thought of spending more time with Katie. "That's okay."

Ned sighed. "I wish you could come here or I could use my partner to execute these documents, but your uncle's will specifically asks for me to execute the documents to you, at the inn."

Roman knew this. "Who is buying the Inn?"

Ned hesitated. "What do you mean?"

"I want to talk to the new owners. I have someone in mind that could take care of the place for them. She doesn't cost much. She's fixing up the place."

"Are you talking about Katie?"

Roman relaxed. Good. Ned knew. "Yes, I want to make sure she's taken care of."

"Uhh…"

"What?"

"Truthfully, I don't know what they have planned and I don't think it's smart to put that kind of stipulation in the contract. They might want to flip it or something."

"Oh." His mind whirled with the ramifications of that for Katie.

"I didn't think you'd mind. You said you just wanted to get rid of it quick."

He felt trapped. "Well…"

"You do still want to sell it, right Mr. Young?"

"Yes." He spoke quickly, immediately thinking of what Katie said about when you answer too fast. "I mean…" Of course he wanted to sell it. What in the world would he do with an inn in Wolfe Creek?

"Mr. Young?"

Frustrated, Roman gripped the phone tighter. He had to get to Katie's house. He didn't want to be late. "Can I call you back, Ned?"

Ned let out another sigh. "I knew this storm was a curse. The buyer really wants this deal. Tell me now if you're having second thoughts."

Being forced to do something he didn't want to do had never been Roman's style. "I'll call you tomorrow, Ned."

He shook his head and looked at himself in the steam of the master bath mirror. He'd only been here for two days, and he felt different. Changed. He thought of his uncle and the last conversation he'd had with him—'Remember, you're good at the game, but the game of life is important too. People are important. Don't give up on love. Don't give up on family. It's the only important thing there is in this life.' Could Wolfe Creek be more? Could Katie be more?

Because there was really no place to stop and get flowers, he stopped at the gas station to get…something.

"Running into Roman Young two times, it must be my lucky day." Behind the register he saw Tiffany, the waitress from earlier.

Feeling caught, he took a step further away from her, toward the candy aisles.

She let out a low whistle. "Wow, you clean up good." She dropped one shoulder and gave him a seductive look.

Truthfully, Tiffany wasn't a bad-looking girl. Pretty even, but her huntress personality did not appeal to him.

"H-hey," he said lamely, scanning the shelves of candy, thinking about what Katie and Josh would like for a treat.

Tiffany moved out from behind the counter. "Whatcha doing?"

He picked up some bubble gum and a couple of candy bars. "Nothing much." Swiftly, he went to the next aisle, taking donuts and popcorn off of the shelves.

She was closing in on him. "I wondered if I'd get a chance to see you again, but if there's one thing you can count on in Wolfe Creek, it's that you always run into people."

"Whether you want to or not," he whispered under his breath. He moved to the counter to pay.

She was behind him. "What was that?"

Roman took an extra step closer to the register, and she took one closer to him. The only thing between them was the junk food, and he held it out like a shield. "Um, nothing. Could I buy this stuff? I'm running late."

Shifting her gaze to all the junk food she snorted. "Do you eat this stuff all the time?"

Heck no. "Yep." He did not want to engage more than he had to in this conversation.

Before he knew what happened, she pulled out a phone and took a picture of him holding all the junk food. "That's crazy!"

Now he was angry. "What are you doing?"

She snapped another picture, and he had to resist the urge to rip her phone out of her hand and throw it to the floor like he did periodically to any paparazzi that taunted him. Truly, this had been the hardest part about being famous—the cameras. He thought about the fact that he hadn't had anyone stalking him to take his picture the past two days and how nice that had been.

"Tiffany," he said gritting his teeth, "you need to put your phone away and let me pay for these please."

Her face turned worried. "Okay." She moved to go behind the counter and started ringing him up. "You know I'm not going to post those or anything. I just want to show my mama and daddy when I get home. My daddy loves the Destroyers. You're his favorite player. He never lost faith in you, even after that horrible hit to your knee."

This softened him.

She swiped his card and gave him a signature receipt to sign and then the real receipt. "I'm sorry. Really. I—I'll delete those pictures right now." She winked at him. "But, let the record show, I've always been team Roman, too." She whispered, "You're much cuter than Dumont. I don't know what your ex-wife was thinking."

He watched her. He took the bag of junk food and sighed. "Why don't you delete those pictures, and I'll do you one better."

"What?"

He nodded. "Come here, and we'll get a selfie together. Then you'll have a real picture to show your parents."

"Eek!" She ran around the counter, her phone already whipped out. "Ohmygosh!" She slammed into his side, already holding up the phone and positioning it.

He let out a soft laugh and put his arm around her, putting on his media smile.

Without warning, and without any malcontent—only complete self-interest—at the last second, Tiffany reached up and kissed his cheek before snapping the picture. "Eek!" She slipped away and giggled. "I'm sorry! I had to!"

He shook his head and went for the door. "Have a good night, Tiffany!"

CHAPTER 9

FEELING EXTREMELY LAME WITH a bag of junk food in his hand, he rang the doorbell of the cute little home that Katie lived in. It was a couple of streets behind Main Street. The home itself looked a little worn, but he noticed the fresh curtains and the spring wreath that hung on the front door.

Josh answered the door, swinging it back wide. He was in superman jammies, and his hair looked damp. "Hi." He ginned up at him. "I can't believe you came." He said a little breathlessly.

Roman bent down and smiled back. "I can't believe you invited me." He copied the breathless way Josh had spoken.

Josh giggled and waved his arm to have him come in. "Come on, Mama made her famous Lasagna, and she made a strawberry spinach salad, and she even made her homemade bread after school." Dramatically, he licked his lips and rubbed his tummy.

Following Josh, Roman's stomach growled. Lasagna and fresh bread sounded delicious. He couldn't remember the last time he'd had fresh bread. Or that someone had made it for him. He flashed back to a memory of standing in the kitchen with his mother. He'd probably been fifteen. Before she'd gotten the news of the cancer. He had this sudden, vivid memory of her holding out mushy bread dough for him.

"Hey." Katie stood in her apple-decorated kitchen. She wore a black turtleneck with jeans, and her hair was long and straight down her back. His breath caught for a second. She'd worn make up, and her eyes looked slightly exotic.

"H-hey." His mouth was dry, and he didn't know why his brain seemed to completely scatter.

She took off the apple apron that she wore and rinsed her hands, smiling at him. "I'm glad you could make it."

For a moment, it felt like she might be slightly off kilter and maybe couldn't catch her breath. But he didn't have much time to think about it.

Josh tugged at the bag in his hand. "What did you bring?" He tried to peek inside.

"Josh." Katie moved around the counter and took his shoulder. "Honey, that's rude."

All Roman could do was smile, delighted by the rawness of kids. He loved kids, taking every chance he'd gotten to do promo work at schools. He squatted down and held the bag open for him. "Well, since I don't have your mom's baking skills, this is what I came up with in a pinch."

Josh's eyes widened. "Holy cow! That's a lot of junk food! Mama never lets me eat all that stuff!"

Roman and Katie locked eyes, both of them smiling at Josh's reaction. Roman handed the bag to Katie. "Your mom can be the boss of it." He gave her a flirtatious wink, acknowledging the inside joke.

She cocked an eyebrow, but kept a grin on her face. She put the bag on the counter. "Let's go sit down for dinner."

"I can't wait for dessert. Let's do dessert first!" Josh pleaded.

Katie gently held him by the shoulder and started moving to the candle lit table in the back of the kitchen. "No spoiling your dinner, like Roman said—for dessert."

Josh did mini jumps. "Can we eat it for movie night, mama?" he asked, slipping into his chair. He jerked back. His eyes alight. "Wait, can Roman stay for movie night?"

Katie motioned for Roman to take a seat then she looked caught. She sat. "Josh, Roman probably doesn't want to stay for Buzz Light Year."

Immediately, Josh swerved to him. "Do you?"

If Josh hadn't wanted him to stay so badly, he would have wondered—by Katie's reaction—if he was wanted at all.

"Please!" He put his hands together in a prayer position.

Roman didn't know what to say. He, once again, looked at Katie for acknowledgement.

She smoothed her clothes and then met his gaze. "Roman, would you like to stay for movie night?"

He nodded. "I'd love to."

"Yay!" Josh clapped.

Katie rolled her eyes. "I'm sorry."

The idea that she should be sorry about how much Josh wanted him there, was the furthest thing from what he was feeling. "No worries."

Her face turned red. "It-it's not you. I mean. Not cause you're famous. He's just been …" she trailed and looked down at her hands.

Suddenly, it hit him. One year. Tomorrow. The poor kid had lost his father one year ago.

"It's my dad." Josh's voice was sad, and he looked down. "He died, ya know."

The center of Roman's chest tightened. He blinked. "I'm sorry."

Josh looked up at him, tears in his eyes. "I know you lost your Uncle Jim. Were you two close?"

At this moment Josh did not seem like a normal seven year old. Roman reached over and put a light hand on Josh's shoulder. "Yes. I ... I wish I would have been even closer to him ..." He trailed for a second. A sudden tear leaked out of him. Roman couldn't believe he was actually losing it. Before coming to Wolfe Creek, he hadn't cried in a long time. Even when he'd caught Sheena cheating. He had been angry, sad, depressed, but he hadn't cried. Now he was crying at the drop of a hat. He brushed a ragged hand over his face. "My mom died a few years ago too."

Josh's face filled with concern. "Well, I guess both of us have parents to miss."

Roman pulled his hand back and leaned over the table, turning to glance at Katie. She had a full stream of tears running down her cheeks. He swallowed back the rest of his emotion and smiled at this seven-year old that seemed a lot older than his age. "Yep."

Katie sniffed and grinned at him.

Roman let out a breath, his heart pounding in his chest. "It's okay to miss them. It's good to miss them."

Josh wiped his face. "Okay, let's eat, mom."

She bowed her head and reached for both of their hands. "Okay, let's pray, then we'll eat."

CHAPTER 10

As quickly as Josh had gotten serious about missing his dad, he flitted to other thoughts, keeping the conversation going through dinner with questions about Roman's childhood, his mother, his father, why he didn't have any brothers.

Roman fired back questions in equal amounts about Josh's teacher, his friends, why he wasn't playing football yet.

At this, Josh rolled his eyes and looked sheepishly at his mother. "She won't let me until I'm twelve."

Katie had an eyebrow cocked when Roman turned to her.

"Well," Roman remembered his own mother having that rule. He also remembered ganging up on her with Uncle Jim. She hadn't given in until he was eleven, after much convincing. He grinned. "Then you'll listen to your mother. They're right most of the time." He winked at Katie.

Josh seemed to think about it. Then he turned to his mother. "Can I have a donut, please mom?"

He'd eaten most of his dinner.

Katie finished chewing and then took a sip of water. "Yes." Her eyes sparkled with happiness as Josh jumped off the chair and ran for the sack.

They both laughed.

Katie's phone buzzed. She got up and checked it.

"Everything okay?" Roman asked.

Giving him her phone, she glared at him. "I see you've already been claimed by your Wolfe Creek Bachelorette."

Even though Roman wasn't surprised to see the selfie of him and Tiffany, he knew he was blushing. "Arg. I let her take a selfie with me at the gas station."

Rolling her eyes, Katie took her phone back. "Well, I guess your image can handle Tiffany."

He was confused. "How come you get tweets from Tiffany?"

"I don't. Tiffany just texted me to make sure I saw it and added the link."

A laugh jerked out of Roman. "Of course she did."

She shook her head.

Roman finished eating. "Well. Thank you for dinner. And you can send out a tweet of our sledding picture anytime you want." He cleared his throat when she glared at him again. "You know, just in case you want to combat Tiffany."

She scoffed, "I wouldn't do that."

He grinned, liking the fact she was still staring at the picture of him. "Well, you don't have to get my attention like that."

"I don't?" she challenged.

He winked at her and stood. "No, Mrs. Winters, you have all my attention."

Katie looked surprised and stood, too. "You're not leaving, are you?"

The fact she looked upset made Roman happy. He gathered his and Josh's dishes. "In my house, whoever cooked never did dishes." That had been his mother's rule, and she'd clung to it hard and fast, even as he'd gotten older. Granted, Sheena had never cooked so it'd never been a thing before.

"Oh no." She began clearing her own dishes and put the salad dressing in the crook of her elbow. "I couldn't let you."

Leveling her with a frown, Roman walked for the sink. "I don't think you have a choice. I'm a guest."

"Exactly," she said, insisting, "Guests don't do dishes." She shoved herself between him and the sink just as he was putting the dishes in.

He pulled his arm back and then put the dishes into the sink with her in front of him. It felt intimate standing so close together. He breathed in her now familiar mellow lemon scent. His heartbeat ratcheted up a notch. He was leaning just a bit, and her lips were right there. At the perfect level.

When he looked back to her eyes, he realized they were on his lips, and she appeared to be breathing just as hard.

"You're not doing dishes. Why do you always have to push me?"

He couldn't help himself. He drew closer, studying her eyes. "It's not pushing. It's manners." His voice was low.

Her breath hitched, and she grinned quickly spinning to the side and putting the dishes down into the sink. She flipped on the faucet. "You're too late, I've already started."

Looking back, he would wonder why he had felt compelled to pick her up and take her into the front room.

She fought against him, but he was too strong. "Roman, put me down!"

"Yeah! Woot!" Josh was beside them, a donut in each hand. "No dishes for you, mom!"

He put her on the couch, but kept her arms pinned to the sides for a second before letting go and sprinting back to the kitchen. He heard trailing laughter.

"He got you, mom!" Josh called out.

She laughed more. "Yes, he did."

Roman had barely begun filling the dishwasher when she came back in. Her chin up, she went straight to the table, a grin on her face. "You are the most *mannered* guest I've ever had."

A laugh escaped him at her backhanded compliment. "Thank you." He focused on cleaning the dishes and putting them in the dishwasher.

She put all the food away and hummed.

"Mom, can I turn the movie on?"

"Go brush your teeth, and then you can." She opened the fridge and put leftovers in. "We'll be out in a second."

It was ridiculous, but being in the kitchen with her and watching her cheerfully put away leftovers, he was filled with more than happiness. He felt content and at home. Then she was done. She took a towel, sliding next to Roman. "Excuse me, I need some water."

Feeling silly, he took some bubbles and put them on her nose. "I guess I can spare some." He pushed the faucet up.

Hesitating, she blew the bubbles off her nose and then gently swiped some more up and onto his nose.

Their eyes met, and all Roman wanted to do at this moment was kiss her. This simple task, sharing a meal on a cold night, and then doing this normal chore left him breathless. How he had wanted something like this with Sheena. How he'd longed for it. But, she'd been a woman that never would have held a tool, let alone made him home made bread. Heck, Katie had done more sincere things for him in two days than his ex-wife had ever done in their three-year marriage. "Katie," he whispered.

For a second, he thought they might kiss.

"Mom."

Both of them were yanked back to reality.

Josh put his hands on his hips. "When are you guys going to come watch the movie?" he asked.

Katie shushed him and took him back into the front room.

Finishing up the dishes and wiping off the counters, Roman wondered how long he could stand being in the room with her and not kissing her.

CHAPTER 11

GETTING SITUATED ON THE COUCH had been an easy task. "Come sit by me," Josh insisted when the kitchen was put away to Katie's specifications. He held out an old football and a marker. "Will you sign this?"

Roman took the football. "How about I make you a deal?"

"Okay." Josh looked at him expectantly.

"How about I give you a signed Cowboy's ball tomorrow?"

He bounced in his seat. "Really?"

He'd seen a ball that his uncle had kept by his bedside, with Roman's signature on it. He was sure his uncle wouldn't mind if Josh had it. "I'll send it home with your mom."

He grinned. "Deal."

Katie sat on the other side of Josh, and they all fell into a silent camaraderie as they watched the movie.

Every couple of minutes Josh pointed at the movie and laughed and asked Roman if he'd seen this part. Roman really hadn't seen it. He relaxed into a comfortable spectator position, crossing his ankle on his knee.

It wasn't too long before Josh lay back and began to doze against his mother's side.

At first Roman tried not to look at Katie. Then not looking at her ended up being the only thing he could focus on. Finally, he relented.

To his immense pleasure, she was already staring at him, her hand on Josh's head and a grin on her face. Her eyes were that bright, almost turquoise green.

"What?" he whispered, feeling caught.

She looked down at Josh for a second. His eyes were closed, and his breathing was steady. "You're not what I expected, Roman Young."

Sudden warmth filled him, and he grinned. He could only imagine what she had thought of him from the media coverage. He lifted his eyebrows. "I guess my only answer is...I never expected you, Katie Winters."

At this, she grinned back.

He nodded to Josh. "Do you want me to carry him up?"

She gave a quick nod.

He stood and then, with extra care, tugged Josh gently from his mother's arms.

Katie went ahead of him, turning on the lights up the stairs.

He followed her into a super hero decorated room with blue curtains and a Destroyers bed spread. He couldn't resist. "This boy is clearly a good boy."

She drew the covers back and sighed. "What can I say? He and his father always liked the Destroyers."

Roman put him in the bed and then backed up as she finished tucking him in. Josh woke a little. "Mama, lay by me."

"Will you turn off the light?" Katie asked as she slipped beside Josh in his bed.

Roman backed up, turning off the light and softly going down the stairs. His mind was filled with her. Her long, soft curls and lemon smell—like lemonade on a summer day on the porch with his mother. Emotions swirled through him that he didn't know how to handle, but they felt good. Real. Everything that his life in Texas was not.

He heard her singing some soft song to Josh. Yes, that was what he liked about Katie. She was real. The kind of woman a man could hold tight on a cold night, without worrying if he messed up her hair. The kind of woman a man could tease and pick up. The kind of woman who would put him in his place—for the right reasons, like to tell him to be kind because Henry and Mrs. K were dealing with a lot.

He sat on her couch and watched Buzz Light Year. It mystified him that suddenly he'd found everything he'd ever wanted. Right here. At the Alaskan Inn.

Had his uncle known that he would fall in love with Katie? How could he have? Maybe he'd hoped? Warmth filled him.

Katie padded down the stairs and Roman felt his pulse spike again. Dang, how is it he couldn't get used to being near her? He had been at the classiest events, on camera shoots, at the best parties and he had never, ever felt nervous around those women. But here, in the middle of podunk nowhere, here was a woman, wearing a tool belt and pom pom hats, that put him off his game.

She stood by the TV and changed the channels, putting on the news. Immediately, sports came up, and his picture splashed onto the screen. She sat down next to him.

"Tonight, in the Dumont/Young show down, our sources say Young went out of town to get out of the media's eyes. Sources say that owner Ty Halstad still wants Young to come back and take his rightful place this year, but there have been grumblings after the big win last week that Young might be done with his game. That..."

Katie picked up a remote and turned the television off.

He hadn't realized that his hands had turned to fists and that he was on the edge of the couch.

Katie put the remote down. "Shouldn't have turned on the news."

He let out a sigh. It felt silly to admit, but he'd almost, for just a few days in Wolfe Creek, forgotten all the troubles back home. "How come the word home suddenly sounds wrong?" He stood and walked in a circle, a small circle in her cute living room that had two big magnetic boards filled with Josh's art pictures. He walked over to study them. She'd already added the picture from earlier.

"I'm sorry, Roman."

He studied the pictures of animals, of her and Josh together, of little things from nature. His heart tugged. The two of them seemed happy. He stopped when he got to the front mantel and saw a picture of her and Josh and her husband, John.

"That's the last picture we have of all of us together." She stood beside him.

Without thinking, he took her hand. "It's beautiful." He studied a few others on the mantel, and then he noticed that her hand had gone still.

He looked down at their hands together. Instantly, he dropped her hand. "I'm sorry."

She blinked and stared up at him with those sad green cat eyes. Beautiful eyes that had so many shades and emotions in them. "I have a question for you."

He studied her back, feeling the chemistry between them. "Only if I can ask a question, too."

A slow grin spread across her face. "Maybe."

He lifted an eyebrow. "Maybe, huh?"

Her face stiffened. "I have a real question."

He let out a breath. "Shoot."

At his concession, she took in a breath and backed up from him, fingering one of her son's pictures. "I can understand why you play football. The rush, the thrill … the money."

"Yes, yes, and yes."

She swerved back. "And, believe me, I know more about your ex-wife and what Jim thought of her than you probably do."

This, he hadn't been expecting. "Okay."

"And I know about the knee and the months you've been rehabbing it."

Unbelievably, this conversation kept getting more and more upsetting. "Okay."

"Here's my question …"

"'Bout time."

She was intense. "Why don't you quit?"

This confused him. He took a step back. "What?"

"Quit. I mean … you've taken them to two championship games. You were on the team this year so you've been a part of three championship games. You've made millions of dollars. Your uncle told me you made smart investments, and I know your ex got half, but you still have assorted businesses …"

Being blindsided on the field, or in business, especially with friends was not something he appreciated. His back straightened. "See, you have the advantage on me, Katie. I have no idea about your financial assets."

At this, Katie let out a light laugh. "I have some death benefits and the paycheck the estate from the inn sends to me." She rolled her eyes. "I have my degree, and I could get a full-time job, but I like the flexibility I have with Josh right now." She shrugged. "Do you think I'm stupid? I think everyone around me thinks I'm stupid for not moving to a city and getting a full-time job, so I don't have to live in this rinky-dink place. My parents even asked me why I'm still here. They want me to relocate to Salt Lake and make myself more marketable." She shrugged again. "But I like being here. I like knowing Henry and Mrs. K and every single person in this town. I like people knowing me, even when it's hard. Even when they give me jobs I don't want." The side of her lip tugged up. "I like that Josh feels safe."

"I don't think you're stupid," he said quickly. "Believe me, that's the furthest thing from my mind."

"Then what do you think?" she challenged.

He didn't reply to that. Instead he said, "I thought I got a question."

Their eyes locked, and all the joking stopped. Her eyes fluttered. "Go ahead."

All at once his palms had turned sweaty, and he wiped them down the sides of his legs like he would if he were in a huddle. His heart pounded, and he still couldn't understand how Katie could put him right on the edge. "I think you're one of the most beautiful, strong, amazing women I've met in my entire life."

Her eyes flashed wider. "That wasn't a question."

A grin formed on his lips. "I was saving it."

She looked away. "You think I'm beautiful?"

Certainty filled him. He took a step closer to her. "I do. And even more beautiful because you don't flaunt it around."

Red colored her face. "I wouldn't even know how to do that. But," she said, looking back at him, "you shouldn't say that."

Taking a chance, he reached for her hand. "I know you've been through a lot."

She frowned and looked down at his knee. "How do you know that next time you get hit it won't be your neck?"

He withdrew from her and turned away. He didn't need to hear this. "We're back to this?"

She let out a long breath. "Roman, I don't care. I just …. I would just think that you're life is more important than football."

This had been the argument made by every mother that ever watched their son play football, his own included. "You don't think

I know the risks?" He was getting mad and didn't know exactly why. He heard about the risks every day, on the news and social media. "You don't think I keep up on my chances with concussions and everything else?"

Her eyes went sad. She took a beat, and then she looked up at him. "My point is you have enough money. Be done. You are still in great shape and have a life in front of you. As your friend, don't go out there and get yourself throttled and have something else happen to you. A knee is nothing, but other things are something." She broke off then flashed her eyes back to him. "I'm not into men dying before they have to."

The light bulb turned on in his head. Of course. Her husband. He hesitated, thinking of how she'd called him her friend. He sized her up. The only thing he knew for sure at this moment was that he wanted to be more than a friend. But even when she said she just thought of him as a friend, she spoke to him more frankly and with more care than anyone had in a long time. His agent, of course, would never want him to quit. Sheena sure as heck hadn't wanted him to stop. Football had been his life, his dream, everything that mattered. It represented everything that mattered. Granted, he did want other things. He wanted a wife that loved him and that he could love. He wanted kids—lots of them. "I wouldn't even know what to be if I wasn't...this."

"Anything."

"Anything?" Roman could not think of himself as doing just anything.

"Well, I do know about this pretty amazing inn." She grinned. "You could stick around and help do some rehab work." She grinned again. "Join the ranks of the over-educated, under- paid."

All the adrenaline from earlier drained out of his system. Slowly, he reached over and held her hand. "Would I have to work for you?"

She let out a light laugh. "I am kind of getting used to you calling me boss."

"There is that." His heart raced, and he couldn't stop himself from looking at her lips. Her perfectly formed lips that wore no make up. Then he looked at her eyes. All he wanted was to kiss her. For her to melt into him.

But he wouldn't do that. Not tonight. Not like this. Tomorrow was the anniversary of her husband's passing. No. No. No.

They stared into each other's eyes. A breath away from kissing.

"Pansy."

"What?" He let out a breath, the trance broken.

She pulled back. "Well I've been standing here, holding your hands, looking in your eyes, giving you all the signs that a girl wants to kiss you. I would have thought that the great Roman Young would have picked up on it."

There it was. There she was. He laughed. Just when he thought she was vulnerable, she snuck up on him.

Shaking a finger at her, he pulled her closer. "If we're going to kiss, I'm going to let you be in charge of it."

The side of her lip twisted up. "Oh yeah?"

He got even closer to her. "Yeah."

Her hand released his, and she ran her hand up his left wrist, his forearm, and then slid it on top of his shoulder. "First I have a question."

He was pretty sure the speed of his heart alone might break one of his ribs. "Another question?"

"How many women have you kissed?"

This he had not been expecting.

She grimaced. "That bad, huh?"

"I …"

She cut him off by putting a gentle finger on his lips. "Never mind, I don't want to know."

"How many have you kissed?" he whispered.

"Thirteen." She answered immediately.

This made him laugh. "I guess you've been ready for that question?"

"You never ask a question you're not ready to answer yourself." She cocked her head to the side. "But that includes Jimmy Smith, my first kiss in grade school.

She was smiling, and he couldn't stop himself from inhaling the lemon scent of her and for holding onto this moment. Granted, he was still looking at her lips.

She nudged him. "Do you want a question?"

No. He wanted to kiss her, but he'd promised to wait for her. His scrambled mind searched for a question. "Do you like Dallas?"

A soft laugh came out of her. "The Destroyers."

"I mean, in general."

"Well, I've actually never been to Dallas. The furthest I've been is Orlando. John and I went there on our honeymoon." She laughed. "Arg, sorry. It always comes back to before, right?"

He laughed, his mind flashing to his life with Sheena before. Katie was so different. He felt like a completely different person being with each of them.

"Penny for your thoughts."

Roman patted his pocket. "No pennies."

She stroked gently down his cheek and then smoothed his hair behind his ear.

He was on fire. He closed his eyes.

"Do you still love her, Roman? Your ex?"

He opened his eyes, the fire chilling at the mention of Sheena. "Honestly, I don't think what Sheena and I had together could be classified as love. I thought it was, but the further away I am from it, the more I see it for what it was."

"What was it?"

"It was fun. All the time fun, and I was caught up in what it meant to be a star football player. But it was empty. I remember thinking, one time, that it felt like we just lived for the cameras. To build her modeling career, to build my brand." He shuddered. "It was empty. Really, really empty."

Then her other hand slid up his right wrist, forearm, and shoulder. He felt himself sigh, and he pulled his hands together behind her waist, pulling her closer, relishing the smell of her. "Hmm."

She laughed. "You sound like you want to eat me."

He cocked his head to the side. "I think you might taste like lemon pie."

She giggled and threw her head back and pulled closer to him.

He couldn't resist her lips much longer. He liked being this close. Within inches, centimeters. Right there. All he had to do was put his lips on hers.

They breathed, the air electric between them.

"Roman," she whispered.

"Yes," he whispered back, lifting his hand and petting it down the hair on her back. "I love your hair, by the way."

"You do?" She smiled, her white teeth perfect, her lips perfectly kissable.

"I do." He waited.

Her eyes squinted shut for a moment. "Can I tell you something?"

"Hmm…Hmm." He was still smoothing her hair down.

Her eyes fluttered. "The therapist said if I had feelings for another man, at some point, that that was normal. That that was good."

His hand stilled on her hair. Suddenly, she seemed scared. He melted inside. "Katie, we don't have to kiss. We can take things as slow as you want."

The side of her lip turned up. "Are you ever nervous playing quarterback, keeping control of the ball?"

He could swear he felt her heartbeat against him. A tremble went through her.

Or had it gone through him? He hesitated. "Last play."

She leaned back to look at him more directly. "What?"

"My uncle Jim used to tell me, even when I was in little league football, you play every play just like it's your last play. As if it is the final play to get the touchdown that will win you the game. If you play like that, then when it is the last play, you won't be nervous."

She grinned. "Is this the last play?"

Roman grinned to match hers. "With you, Katie Winters, I'm having to play every play my hardest, but I'm hoping this one will lead to a touchdown."

She cocked her eyebrow. "Touchdown?"

He sighed. "Okay, at least a first down."

She laughed and looked at his lips. "Let's find out."

A sudden knock sounded at the door.

Katie jolted back, as if she'd been woken from a trance. She quickly flew to the door. "Oh, goodness." She tugged it back, the cold air instantly making the room uncomfortable. "I completely forgot."

Lou stood there. In Carhartt gear, a beanie cap on his head and large black gloves, his eyes went to Roman and then back to Katie. "Oh, I didn't realize I'd be interrupting."

"It's fine. Come in." Katie's voice had gone from whispered and vulnerable a second before to steady.

He took a step in, keeping his eyes on Roman. Roman stood straighter, not being rude, but sure as heck not offering to make the man anymore comfortable. His thoughts whirled. Were Katie and Lou a thing? He thought he'd detected something between them back at the diner, but she'd said nothing about his slight possessiveness.

Lou looked around, took a long sniff. "Dinner? You made him dinner on movie night?"

Roman watched the scowl that darkened Katie's face, and, when she turned back to him, he saw her cheeks were red.

"Stop it, Lou. We're friends, okay. And you and I are friends, too."

"*Friends*." Lou grimaced. "I was here when your husband died." His jaw clenched. "Dang it, Katie, I was his best friend. And you're here with him when tomorrow ..." His voice trailed and Roman saw the emotion in Lou's eyes.

Now Katie's cheeks weren't just red, they were flaming red. She turned to face Roman. "I'm sorry."

Going for his jacket, Roman nodded his head. "No problem. Thank you for dinner, and tell Josh I'll give him that football tomorrow."

She opened the door and whispered to him as he moved past. "I guess sometimes it's better not to know how that last play will go?"

He stopped, their eyes meeting. "No, it's always better to make the play."

CHAPTER 12

HE LAY IN THE SLEEP NUMBER bed and looked out the window at the crisp night. Mrs. K had stopped by earlier with a tinfoil-covered plate. When he'd admitted that he'd been to Katie's for dinner, she'd only responded with a wink and then put the leftovers in the fridge for the next day.

She'd stayed for twenty minutes, and they'd sat at the big oak table talking about Henry and her children. He realized how normal it had all felt.

How like … home.

Now, he felt lonely. Honestly, even when he was married to Sheena, he'd been lonely. Alone in his thoughts. Granted, he and Sheena had had an amazing physical relationship, but…they'd never really been friends.

Not really.

Okay, after the divorce had he missed having someone to go to dinner, the movies, and assorted social engagements with? Yes. But he hadn't really missed Sheena.

He thought about the past two days with Katie. They'd connected. Laughed. Teased. Played. She felt like his friend.

She *was* his friend, he realized. Maybe the only real friend he had.

His thoughts drifted to Katie again. How she'd tricked him into carrying up the tube. Every. Single. Time. Okay, he hadn't always been tricked, and it had been fun.

The sound of her laugh had made him do the craziest things.

They'd become something more. It wasn't just that he was attracted to her. Majorly attracted to her. No. It was something … he sat straight up in bed. He was in love with her.

It shouldn't be such a surprise to him, but it was. He hadn't been expecting this at all.

He shoved back the covers and stared out the window. It was two am, but he didn't care. That's what agents were for. He pushed Jake's number.

He answered on the second ring. "What are you doing calling me at this hour?"

"You said I could call anytime, rain or shine. Wasn't that your corny sale when I first signed on with you?"

He heard the sound of covers shuffling.

"What are you doing, Jake?"

"Oh, well, I'm sleeping! Sheesh, but since I have you on the phone, let's talk. So, you'll be coming back the day after tomorrow for the meeting, right? Got it lined up for four o'clock. Do you have your flight booked?"

"No."

"You don't have your flight?"

"No."

"Well, I'm getting you one."

"No. Wait. I don't know."

"What do you mean, you don't know?"

He sighed and thought of how her hands felt in his. How lovely she smelled. How Josh loved donuts, and how they'd both had parents that'd died on them. "I may need a couple more days with this snow. Can you reschedule with the owners?" Honestly, he couldn't believe he felt so calm about this.

Jake let out what could only be compared to a Star Trek Klingon war cry. "Do I need to send a helicopter to this podunk … I don't know. Where are you? C'mon, the owners keep saying they're ready to announce who's going to lead the pack next year. I think it's you. I feel it in my bones."

Roman didn't answer, only paced the freezing porch. "What if I got out? What would that mean?"

"Out? You're at the top of your game."

He looked down at his knee. "What if it's more than a knee next time?"

"What are you talking about? Is this about your uncle? About death and dying? C'mon, man, you're not going to die! Look at you, you're in the best shape of your life."

Roman listened to his agent continue giving the speech. The one all players and agents gave. The one about being ten feet tall and superman. Nothing would happen. There were things in the contract in case it did happen. But it wouldn't.

It was strange. For the first time since reading his uncle's letter and thinking about what more to life than football looked like, he could actually see a vision of what that could be. And that vision involved Katie Winters and the Alaskan Inn.

CHAPTER 13

THE NEXT MORNING HE GOT UP EARLY. When he checked his watch, it was 6:30. He hopped out of bed. He needed to run, to do something physical. He got on his snow clothes and went to the barn, the big one with the radio. He started stacking that huge dumped pile of wood where Katie had mentioned it needed stacking.

Of course, once he thought of her, he couldn't quit thinking of her. Katie. Strong, like a marathon runner with lean muscles. Very feminine. Her eyes sparkled, but they were also sometimes sad, especially when she didn't know he was looking at her.

He thought of her husband's grave and the picture of them on the mantel. Their family. He sighed, feeling somewhat sad himself. He would never be that man to her. Then he was immensely irritated. Why was he even thinking about that?

All the thoughts that had passed through his mind last night were ridiculous. Why would he willingly give up a chance to finish out his career? Well, he wouldn't. He was here to sell this place. When the stupid attorney got through the snow, he would sign the papers. His uncle's wishes would be satisfied—he'd come, he'd seen, he'd go. Back to his life.

The pictures from her mantel crept back into his mind. Frustrated, he went through the Carhartt pockets, pulled out his phone, and streamed some rock music, but thoughts of her came back. She hadn't looked as thin in her pictures as she looked now. She was too thin in his mind. Not that he didn't understand a woman's drive to be thin. Sheena had been obsessed with it. That's part of the reason she never cooked, claiming she didn't want to get fat. But not Katie. No, all he could say after the meal last night was that girl could cook. His stomach grumbled as he thought of the homemade bread.

He thought of sledding with her. They'd had fun yesterday. He paused and wiped the sweat off his forehead. That was more fun than he'd had in as long as he could remember. A nervous stir went through him as he thought about Lou. He hefted a large piece of wood across the barn and then immediately laughed at his Neanderthal behavior. He was jealous of a man that he hardly knew anything about.

A tap on his shoulder sent him jumping, dumping wood all over the place.

"What's up, QB?" High-pitched laughter sounded through the air.

Katie. She stood there, smiling like a kid on Christmas.

Glaring at her, he threw his hands up. "Is that how you get your kicks?"

She laughed harder. She jumped up and down and wiped tears from the edges of her eyes. "I don't think I've ever seen anything so funny."

"Oh yeah." He would think she would feel bad about him being scared to death and dumping half the load he'd stacked, but she was so happy. And, for some dumb reason, that made the center of his chest happy.

She peeled off her snow clothes and he saw she was dressed like normal—yoga pants, but this time she wore a faded Destroyers t-shirt. "So I guess we're working on stacking this woodpile today?"

He picked up more wood. "Nice shirt."

Throwing a piece of wood on the stack, she lifted a shoulder. "Thought I'd give it a shot."

Warmth filled him. He watched her; not even trying to stop the grin that he was sure filled his whole face. "So how was Lou last night?" He was trying to bring it up in a very casual way, but it already felt awkward.

Scrunching up her nose, she nodded to the scattered wood. "Can we just work for a bit?"

Silently conceding, he picked up a piece of wood and threw it toward the stack. They both worked side by side for about twenty minutes. She worked hard, which made him work all the harder just to prove that he wouldn't be outdone.

"Thanks again for last night." He paused and wiped his forehead in between chucking things.

She threw another piece of wood. "I'm glad you came. Josh had a good time."

Of course he noticed that she'd said Josh, not her. Lou's face flashed into his mind. "Josh is a good kid." It was true. He liked him.

At talk of Josh, she smiled. "He is."

"You've done a good job." He threw another piece of wood on the stack.

Taking care to go around his path where he was throwing all the wood, she moved toward him. "Thank you for being interested in him. He can't wait to show all the kids his ball—signed by the great Roman Young."

He paused. "It's in the inn on the table." He hadn't wanted to forget to give it to her.

She nodded, reaching for a water bottle and then taking a long sip. "Honestly, Josh has done exceptionally well. I think possibly because I was such a wreck after his dad …" she trailed off.

Today. The day he'd died. He sobered. "What happened?"

She hesitated. "I told you how your uncle started paying me before I started working."

He nodded.

"Well, I don't know what I would have done without that money. I … was lost, you know. For a few months I just went through the motions—taking Josh to school, clean the house, get dinner, then get in bed and set my alarm for when school would be out. If I hadn't had Josh …. I don't know what I would have done." Tears budded in her eyes then she shook her head. "Anyway …"

He scoffed, "Then you maniacally threw yourself into the inn." He was getting it now. Why this place was so important to her.

She stared at him and then laughed. "I guess so." She wagged her finger. "That's what I like about you."

Not taking the compliment well, he knew he was blushing. "Thanks, but I don't say it like it is all the time."

She laughed again. "You're pretty honest for a football player."

Instantly, he thought about the fact he'd been lying to her, at least not telling the whole truth, he reasoned. "Not really."

"No, seriously, it's been really great to have you here the past few days. I think the anticipation of something is always harder then the actual thing, don't you?" She continued. "If I can get through today, then I'll be good." She blinked away more moisture in her eyes.

Before he could stop himself, he pulled her into a hug. "You will. You'll be just fine, Katie Winters."

Staying against him for a few seconds, he could feel her taking deep breaths.

Then she pulled away. "You know I've seen the media stuff on you, and I think that all gets blown out of proportion."

Now he knew he was getting red. Regret coursed through him. "It wasn't all a lie. I have done things I'm definitely not proud of."

She frowned. "My advice is to go easier on yourself. That's what I learned from my therapist. Let yourself off the hook sometimes. Guilt, anger, and regret can eat you alive. Just put your head down and work hard, that seems to help more than anything."

Guilt tugged at his conscience. She thought he was a good man. He should tell her he was planning on selling the inn, but, selfishly, he wanted to spend one last day with her before she knew. "Let's go get lunch."

She glanced down at her sport's watch. "It's not even ten."

"Exactly, I haven't eaten today, and you're too skinny."

She rolled her eyes. "Whatever."

CHAPTER 14

LUNCH WAS AT A PIZZA PLACE. One that was attached to the ski resort. It was far more posh then The Lizard Café or the Wolfe's Haven. This place was all stainless steel tables and chairs. Black, sleek, leather couches around gas lit fireplaces. Framed, watercolor art lined the walls. Roman thought about how Sheena loved to bid on stuff like this. His house was filled with meaningless shapes and colors. He hated it.

Katie had turned to him on the way inside and shrugged. "This place doesn't feel homey at all, but it has the best pizza in town."

A couple of skiers were sitting around, drinking coffee, still wearing their boots on their feet. Most of them were just taking breaks between runs.

They went to an open table next to a huge window that overlooked the side of the mountain. A waitress took their order and Roman couldn't help feeling disappointed when the news guy on the large flat screen above them announced the roads up to Wolfe Creek would be cleared by the end of the day and available to skiers.

She faced him, taking off her coat. "You're probably glad about the roads."

He took a sip of water and flashed her a grin. "Why would you say that?"

"So you can get back. This town has probably felt ... small."

The way the sun hit her hair and her green eyes looked so open and happy to be just sitting here with him made him wish he could lean over and take her hand. She was beautiful. No make-up. No glamour. Everything about her was beautiful. She wore her hair back in a braid down the back of her neck. Sitting here in her Destroyers t-shirt, she looked younger than last night. His heartbeat picked up speed. "Actually, I've really enjoyed being here. You look good today, by the way."

Immediately, she frowned and then looked out the large glass windows to the side of them that gave a nice view of the ski resort. "You've got your big meeting with the owners tomorrow, right?"

This took him by surprise. It shouldn't have. Granted, the media was covering it pretty intensely. "Hmm. Yeah." He hesitated. "But you do look good," he insisted.

She still didn't look at him. "Roman, I don't think you should be complimenting me like that. I mean … especially since today and everything."

How could he be so stupid? "I'm sorry," he said quickly. Stupid. Stupid. Stupid. He was hitting on her on the anniversary of her husband's death.

It was only awkward for a couple of minutes. Then she looked back at him. "So, do you think the owners will put you back as a starter?"

"I thought you thought I shouldn't even play."

"I don't." She grinned. "But I may or may not have checked Google last night."

Happiness filled him. "Really?"

"Don't get a big head, QB," she scoffed.

Typical of what he'd come to expect between them, they simply stared into each other's eyes for a few seconds. It felt completely strange to him how normal things felt with her. Almost like destiny. Like they were meant to meet. "You still haven't told me what happened with Lou."

"Do you like it there? In Dallas?"

He knew she was avoiding the question, but he let her. Leaning back in his chair, he stretched out his legs and held his water glass. "I love Dallas." That was the honest answer. Sizing her up, he took a sip. "Would you ever leave?"

"Wolfe Creek?" She jerked to attention.

He grinned. "Or shall we say—Mecca, the homeland?"

She let out a breath. "My parents want me to. They keep asking why I'm still here." She shrugged. "You know, the whole over qualified to be an 'inn keeper.'"

At this point, and for some unknown reason, her response meant a lot to him. His heart raced, and he felt like he was on the sidelines waiting to go back in the game. "So would you leave?" he repeated.

The moment went slow, and their eyes locked. Something passed between them. Some kind of energy that took his breath away. She looked vulnerable and like the only thing that she might want ... could be him. Then she looked down. "No."

No. No? "No?"

Their eyes met again, and she set her jaw. "This is Josh's home. I don't have a husband to make decisions with anymore. To be anchored to, but I have this place. I want to give Josh that stability. So I'll stay here."

Nervous jitters went through him. Somewhere—deep down, he'd known this. "I can understand that. Is it because of Lou?"

Their food was set on the table. They each pulled off a hot pepperoncini bite. "So good," Roman commented.

"Right," she agreed, eating heartily.

"Well …?" He wasn't going to give up hearing what had happened with Lou. It felt silly but he did want a chance to know.

She took another bite. "He … he likes me. He wanted to make his intentions 'officially' known last night." She air quoted.

This mystified Roman. "Wow, that's—"

"Gentlemanly," she filled in for him and lifted her chin.

A small breath puffed out of him. "That's exactly what I was going to say."

She laughed.

"So he hasn't made a move on you before?" he probed, taking a bite of pizza and wondering why he felt like he was competing for her.

She hesitated and then let out a long breath. "He's made a move before, but honestly, I was completely uninterested then. So we decided to wait a year. As he mentioned, he was my husband's best friend. It kind of felt natural for him to be around after everything. He helped me out a lot. Then he started coming over sometimes."

"On movie night," Roman filled in for her.

She rolled her eyes. "I should have thought he'd be coming over, sorry."

Waving his hand in the air to dismiss her worry, he took another bite of pizza.

"A couple of months ago I asked him to lay off on the 'dating me' bit. I guess he looked at last night as a chance to start dating again. Officially."

"Oh." Roman tried not to ask too many questions. Like, why she had to ask him to lay off if she was ready to pursue other relationships now. His heart kept pounding at an unsteady rate. Dang, he felt like a teenager. "Hmm." He tried to sound casual, disinterested. He wasn't interested. He was going back to Dallas and she was ... here.

A mischievous glint came into her eyes. "What?"

He sniffed and wiped his face with a napkin. "Nothing."

"You're not saying something."

"Nothing," he answered quickly.

Cocking an eyebrow, she nodded. "So you're just asking ... as a boss."

He pointed at her. "Exactly. I just want to know if he can fix things."

The look she gave him told him she wasn't completely convinced. "So are you keeping me on?"

He stared at her, not comprehending for a second. "What?"

"As the manager?"

Her eyes looked bright and hopeful. Instantly he decided he would only sell it to someone who agreed to keep her on as the manager. He would make sure that was in there. "Of course."

She nodded. "Thanks."

Looking for another subject, he pointed to the ski lift. "You ski?"

She scoffed, "I could put you to shame, QB."

Grateful that she'd picked up on his discomfort, he fell back into the playful banter. "You talk big, boss."

She winked at him. "I'm pretty sure I can take a Texas boy." She looked thoughtful. "But I don't have skies...or a pass."

He frowned, wondering at the difference between her and the other women he'd dated. They'd always just assumed he would pay. Always assumed he would not only pay, but also buy them things. "C'mon, let's go get outfitted. I'll tell you what. I'll pay if you make me a bet."

She laughed. "I don't think I have much you want."

This was just the thing he wanted. "If you win, I'll cook dinner for you and Josh. If you win, you cook."

Eyeing him, she shoved the pizza away. "I would say you just want to get out of work ... if you didn't own the place."

He grinned. "What do you say?"

She frowned. "I can't tonight."

Lou's face flashed through his mind. "Oh, I see."

Her face went blank. "It's not that. Lou, I mean."

"What?" There was no way he was blushing. No way. "It's fine."

She looked thoughtful. Then she exhaled. "Josh's grandparents have asked for him to come stay for the night."

"Oh." His mind whirled. "Well, I guess it could just be you and me."

Then he saw her blush. "I just need to be alone tonight."

Disappointment surged within him. "Oh." He tried to recover and stood. "I understand."

She stood. "I'm sorry."

He pulled a couple bills from his wallet and left them on the table, trying to cover the let down. "It's fine." All he could think about was the fact he was leaving tomorrow. "No big deal." He would just enjoy this moment. With his friend.

Katie grinned and stood. "C'mon, QB, I can school you and still get a few hours of work in."

Warmth surged inside of him. "Let's go."

CHAPTER 15

ROMAN SAT IN THE HOT TUB ON his uncle's deck. How he needed the hot tub. They'd spent the afternoon on the slopes. She'd taken it easy on him on the bunny hill. Then she'd blown him away on the real slopes. Good thing she hadn't taken him up on the bet. He didn't know how he would have cooked tonight.

At least, that was the lie he was telling himself. The snow had completely stopped, but the view off his uncle's deck took his breath away. With the weather clear, he could see the mountain and the ski resort. He could see little people skiing down the mountain. The sun was setting, and it was breathtaking. Still. Quiet.

It was unusual for him not to check his phone every couple of minutes. Or check facebook or twitter or some news report. But he hadn't today. He'd turned off his phone at lunch, and he hadn't bothered to turn it back on.

The fact that he'd been so consumed with coming to Wolfe Creek and getting the Alaskan sold felt like something from a long time ago. It seemed less important now. It was more important to make sure Katie was taken care of in that contract.

He could keep it if he had to.

The thought had crossed his mind over the past couple of days, but he'd always rejected it. The only thing that would be hard was if he had to see Katie 'officially' dating Lou when he came for visits. She and Lou would get married, have some kids …. He had to quit thinking along those lines or else he would get really depressed. Plus, even if it hurt, he would do it for Katie.

After getting out of the hot tub, taking a long shower, he began looking for his clothes bag.

Folded nicely on the bed were all his clothes he'd worn. There was a note on top of them. "Thought Katie would be working you. Mrs. K."

Warmth flooded him. This lady, that was battling cancer, was doing his laundry just to help him. For some insane reason, tears filled his eyes. She'd insisted he couldn't pay her for cooking and now this. What had Katie said about her the other day? That Mrs. K needed a miracle, and it broke her heart to think she might not get one.

Putting on the clothes, he held onto her note and then pushed it into his wallet, making a decision to have money wired to her account when he got back. "You never know when miracles show up, Mrs. K."

He put on heavy socks and went downstairs. He knew there were leftovers in the fridge, but he wanted to sit by the fire for a bit. He'd started it before he'd gotten into the hot tub and now he put on another log on.

Sitting on the couch, he reflected how nice it had been to check out of the media for a bit. To just … live in the moment. He thought about what Katie had said earlier, about how next time it could be his neck. She'd been right. It could be. It was the fear that stayed on the edges of all football players—that they would get hurt and not be able to play any longer. She'd been right about the fact that he did have plenty of money. He had also been buying up car dealerships and real estate. If there had been anything he'd learned growing up poor, it was that he never wanted to be poor again.

But he did love the game. The competition was the thing that kept him pushing himself the past six months after the injury. He liked being the best. He liked the media attention. Well, he thought of Sheena, maybe he didn't like it as much anymore.

He felt different. Not just from his uncle passing, but also from being here the past few days. He felt like he'd had a snapshot of what close to normal might be able to be.

He leaned forward and held out his hands to the fire, ignoring the tugging hunger inside him. He wished Katie were here. Then he felt bad for wishing it. She needed to be alone. He got that. She missed her husband. Missed someone who had built a life with her—through sweat and worry and with love. An ache burned into him. She'd had love. That's why she'd had a hard time getting out of bed. Why she'd had to see a therapist. Because she knew what real love was.

A tear went down his cheek. It wasn't pity that he felt for the relationship he'd had with Sheena. No. It had been stupidity on his part. Sheena had never pretended to be something other than she was. She had never pretended to be like Katie. It was him that had been different. That felt different now.

Out of nowhere, there was a knock at the door.

CHAPTER 16

PADDING ACROSS THE FLOOR, his heart raced. It could be Mrs. K, but somehow he knew it wasn't. Right or wrong, he hoped it was Katie. He pushed the door back.

There she stood in her Carhartt suit with her red hair in soft curls spilling out of the hat. She pointed to her lips. "I don't know why I put on lipstick, so don't ask."

"Hey." He didn't know what to say, how to act. She was emotionally fragile, and this was the date of her husband's death.

Pushing inside, she shoved a bag into his arms. "You shouldn't stand there and hold the door open. Don't you know it's cold out there?"

He backed up, shaken from his daze and took the bag. "Hey."

She pulled off her snow clothes and hung them up, tugging off her hat. Her cheeks were rosy, and he closed his eyes for a second and inhaled her lemon scent.

Hesitating next to him, she lifted her brow and shrugged. "I thought you might need dinner." She took the bag back and moved toward the kitchen.

He followed and watched how she pulled out a couple of foil-covered containers: salad, chicken, and rice that smelled incredible. He couldn't deny he was hungry, but the hunger he felt wasn't just for food. No. Once he'd seen her at the door, another hunger had stirred inside of him.

She ignored him, setting the table for two. Lighting two candles. She glanced back at him. "Will you light the fire in here?"

He did as he was told, his hands shaking. He didn't know what was going on, but all he could say was that it was something bigger than him. That's all he knew.

She waited at the table, and he noticed she wore a green, emerald turtleneck. With the red hair and lipstick, she looked like a model. Not Sheena kind of model—too perfect, overly done up—no, she looked like an American Girl doll. Pretty. Innocent. Happy.

"Sit," she commanded.

He sat.

After sitting, she picked up her fork. "Aren't you hungry?"

He started eating, not knowing why he was so nervous.

"You haven't said a word," she said.

His throat felt dry. He took a sip of water. "Thank you, this looks great."

She grinned and flipped her hair over her shoulder.

He thought, again, how she was attractive without trying to be. "I'm glad you're here," he whispered without knowing why.

She watched him eating then took a sip of water. "I sat at my kitchen table with a bowl of cereal. Uneaten. I mean, why should I cook if it was just me, right? A night off. Then I realized something."

He put his fork down. "What?"

She put her hand on top of his. "I didn't want to be alone right now."

His heart pounded inside his chest. What was happening?

She laughed. "Don't give me that look, I'm not throwing myself at you or anything."

"I didn't think that," he answered too quickly.

She laughed harder and pulled her hand back to take a sip of water and wipe her mouth. "Yes, you did."

He laughed, too. "Okay, maybe I did, but I wouldn't have let you."

A look of disbelief washed over her face. "You wouldn't have *let* me?"

A serious ache formed into his gut. "No, I wouldn't have let you tonight."

She sobered and blinked. "Thank you. I just didn't want to sit there by myself. I thought …" she broke off and shook her head. "Never mind."

Gently, he took her hand and laced his fingers through hers. "You thought right."

She smiled, and how long they stared at each other, he didn't know. But he did know that he'd been right earlier. Somehow, by destiny or fate, or he'd been brought to the Alaskan Inn to meet Katie Winters.

She teased him about smelling so good, and he teased her about smelling like lemon.

"That's my splurge, I get that lotion when I go into Ogden. It makes me feel feminine."

For some reason, seeing her so vulnerable, her hand in his, made his desire to kiss her go, on a scale of zero to ten, from a strong eight to an eleven or twelve. "You don't need the lotion to be feminine."

They cleaned up, and then he offered to make some of the cocoa that he'd found on the counter. He knew it had to be left from Mrs. K.

"The great Roman Young makes hot cocoa?" She teased him as she put the dishes back into the cupboard.

He tsked his tongue and pulled out some mugs and filled them with hot water from the microwave. "Are you kidding? You're going to get a Young specialty."

"Okay." Katie laughed, and they took their mugs and moved into the living room.

He saw the football on the table in the front room. "Don't forget that for Josh."

She picked it up, and tears came to her eyes. "The one you gave Jim?"

He nodded. "It's from my first season when I took them to the championship game. It's a collector's item."

"Thank you."

The sun had gone down, and they went to the couch. He got one of the heavy quilts and put it over their legs.

She sipped the cocoa. "It's good."

He grinned and sipped his own. "It is good."

Looking at the walls, she let out a breath. "I'm thinking when we remodel this room, we keep some things."

He shrugged and gestured with the cup to the mantel of the fireplace. "Like that old rifle? No, I say take it all down. Get rid of it all and buy new stuff."

She cocked an eyebrow. "You do know that that gun belonged to … let's see … your great, great, great, great grandfather that fought in the Civil War."

The fact she knew more about his history than he did didn't surprise him. "I didn't know that."

Shaking her head, she smiled. "Plus, it was important to Jim. That's enough reason to keep it."

Then he reached for her hand. "Then we'll keep it."

She grinned. "We're agreed then."

"Did I ever have a choice?"

She laughed.

He couldn't explain how much he wanted to be with her, but how much more important it was for him to be there for her tonight. This was her husband's night. Tonight, he would be her friend. So he asked about him. About them.

"Are you sure you want to hear this?"

He did. "Of course."

So she told him. About growing up together. Falling in love their senior year. Marrying right out of high school and leveraging everything to buy the farm.

She sighed. "We made a good team. I was good at keeping the finances organized. He was good with the animals, and we both worked hard." She looked suddenly sad.

He tried to lighten it. "I can see you being good at being organized … or bossy." He took another sip.

She blinked back tears. "I loved him so much, but …" She looked away from him. "The last couple of days with you it's been …" She stopped and shook her head.

Carefully, he put down his cocoa and reached up and touched her hair. "What?"

She put down her cocoa and took his hand and pressed it to her cheek. "Is it bad that I wanted to kiss you last night?" She sucked in a breath. "I'm sad to lose him, I've mourned him for a year, but … I can't deny these feelings for you."

He wouldn't do this. He wouldn't lean forward. He wouldn't do the only thing he'd been thinking about all evening. He sucked in a breath and closed his eyes.

"Pansy."

His eyes flicked open. "What?"

"You're afraid."

This was unbelievable. "Of what?"

"Kissing me." She put her chin out in that challenging way.

He broke off, laughing. "I cannot believe you just said that."

"Well, then you tell me, QB."

The fact that his heart rate sped up, like he was about to throw a pass, did not mean a thing. "It's his day," he whispered.

Katie stayed almost nose-to-nose with him. She stared into his eyes. "I know … and I know I shouldn't want this."

"But you do?"

She blinked, and a tear fell down her cheek. "I want you to kiss me. That's all I know."

He leaned forward. His lips touched hers softly. So softly it could have been a whisper. But he was startled when she put her arms gently around his neck and pulled him closer, deepening the kiss. Her hands ran through his hair, lighting small fires everywhere she touched.

Within the duration of that kiss his whole life passed before him. The life he could have here. With her. With Josh. With, he was shocked to see, a passel of kids around them. They were here in this inn—welcoming families. Possibly skiing together, sledding, going out to the diner, snuggled up by the fire on cold nights.

Then she pulled back, dragging him back to real life.

The side of her lip tugged up. "You have lipstick all over your face." She jumped up. "Let me get you a towel."

Putting his hands on her hips, he tugged her back down. "Huh, uh."

She fell into him, giggling. "Sheesh."

He pressed his lips back to her. "I like lipstick all over my face." He lifted his head back to get a view of her face. "Hey, you have lipstick all over your face, too."

She giggled, and he kissed her more, pulling her closer, relishing the smell of lemon.

The next thing he knew, he had his hand on her cheek and was gently tracing her jawbone.

She tugged back. "I'm sure glad I didn't shoot you the other night."

He laughed and gently kissed her forehead. "I'm glad you didn't shoot me, too."

He got up and put another log on the fire and then went back and snuggled back into her arms, just holding her close. It felt amazing. He never wanted to leave this place.

"So, how did that play go?"

He caught the teasing look on her face, and he grinned. "I'd say we definitely made a first down."

"Oh yeah?" she challenged.

"Well," he caressed her neck and gave her a little kiss on the lips. "But remember every play has to be considered, thought out, fought for." He kissed her again.

She giggled. "Well, don't be thinking you'll move that ball too far, Mr. Young."

He kissed her again. "You mean because of Lou."

After jerking back, she laughed even harder. "Whatever."

Pulling her forward, he gave her another soft kiss. "Tell me, how many kisses has he gotten in?"

A roll of laughter rushed out of her. "And now you've revealed yourself as just another competitive jock."

"Hey." He yanked back, slightly offended. "I do not consider you a game. This is not a game to me."

Her cheeks flushed. "I'm going to be real honest with you, Roman. I don't know if my heart can take it if it's not real."

He gently kissed her, pushing her hair back. "Well, then let's do as Uncle Jim always said. Let's look at every chance we're together like it could determine the rest of the game. Let's make it good."

She wagged her finger. "But no touchdowns, yet." Another blush.

He grinned. "No, we'll save that part."

"You're a good man, Roman Young, even if you've distracted me out of work the past two days."

He sighed. "I know. I'm sorry."

She sighed. "It's okay."

As they watched the fire and held hands, and he was filled with more hope and more love and more joy in that one moment than he'd been in his entire life.

Then, there was another knock at the door.

CHAPTER 17

ROMAN WAS STUNNED TO SEE two men at the door. One man was holding a briefcase with an overcoat and a hat on his head. He knew who it was, and he felt like someone had slammed him in the gut.

The man pushed forward and waved the other man in. "Mr. Young." He stuck his hand out to shake, completely out of breath. "I am so sorry that it has taken so long to get here. The weather here is so unpredictable, and I couldn't get a hold of you all day to let you know that I was bringing the new owner with me. Meet Mr. Stone. He's from back east, but he jumped at the chance to get this Inn." The man was clearly nervous and talking too fast.

Roman didn't have a chance to get a word out before Katie had popped up off the couch, her red hair already rising off of her like a fierce tornado getting ready to strike. "What?"

"Katie—"

Roman moved toward her, trying to take her hand, but she yanked it away and was already squaring off in front of the attorney and the other man.

"You're the new owner?" She accused them and then flung back to Roman. "You never planned to keep it?"

If the look of betrayal on her face at that moment could have been bottled and used against an army, Roman was sure one bottle of it alone could have stopped the Crusades.

"Wait, just listen!"

But she was already pulling on her snow clothes and pushing her pom pom hat down onto her head. "Don't." Her voice had that severe edge to it. The same edge she'd used the first time he'd met her.

"Katie, just stop and listen, please."

Mr. Burcher didn't take a hint, instead he began rambling, "Well, I do have it right, Mr. Young? You did want the new owner here as quick as you could—didn't you? I know you have to get back for the owner's meeting tomorrow, your agent called me pretty insistent that we get this deal done."

Katie pushed past them, then stopped and turned back, her beautiful eyes sad and hurt and vulnerable for a second. She glared at Roman. "Yes, why don't you get the deal done and then get back to your real life, Mr. Young."

Before he knew what'd happened, she was off on the snowmobile, flying down the road.

"Mr. Young? Is everything okay?" Mr. Burcher pressed.

It took nearly five minutes to explain the situation to Mr. Burcher and Mr. Stone. Truth be told Roman knew he should feel bad that Mr. Stone had flown all the way out to make the deal happen, but as he put on his snow clothes and took off after Katie, he could only feel one thing...

Remorse.

That he hadn't told her from the beginning. That he'd selfishly wanted to spend time with her. Then when he'd decided he could keep it, he hadn't taken the time to call poor Mr. Burcher and let him know the change of plans.

Selfish. Selfish. Selfish. Everything Katie had said about him in the beginning. Yes, that is exactly what he was. He hadn't given any of them the courtesy of being honest.

He swung around the corner, hoping to catch her before she was too angry, before things got too blown out of proportion.

He would just explain. Yes, he'd been an idiot. Yes, he'd been selfish. Yes, she was right about him.

But—he'd changed. He wanted to change. He wanted to be with her. He had to have that. He didn't know how, but he would work it out. They could work it out together.

When he pulled up and found her locked in a kiss with Lou took on her front porch, to say that he'd been taken off guard would be like saying that an earthquake leveling a house was a simple inconvenience.

CHAPTER 18

WHEN THE LIGHTS FROM HIS snowmobile hit the door, Katie jerked back from Lou.

If Roman could have seen the wild, crazed look in her eyes, or the bewildered look on Lou's face, it might have appeased him.

But he hadn't been able to see anything other than her kissing Lou.

She blinked into the lights. "Roman?"

But he was already turning the snowmobile to make a circle and head back to the street. Of course the woman that he'd thought he'd fallen in love with was in a lip lock with small- town -ex-husband's- best -friend. She was right, it couldn't get any more cliché in this town.

Red was the only thing he could see as he sped off.

"Roman!" she yelled behind him.

If he had been a smart man, he would have called Mr. Burcher and had him come back and sign the papers on the spot.

But what could he say? The only thing Roman did was pack his bags and leave a note for Mrs. K.

He called his agent.

"Hello, Roman, are you ready to come back?"

"Get me a taxi, and book me a flight out of here ASAP!"

CHAPTER 19

6 months later

HE'D BEEN OFFERED THE POSITION.

As starter.

The great Roman Young would lead his team to another championship game victory.

As he stepped out onto the field for the first pre-season game and took in the crowd, the music, and the energy, none of it felt like it used to.

Her face flashed into his mind.

A reporter shoved a microphone at him. "We're here with Roman Young, first-string quarterback for the Destroyers. Mr. Young, after the hotly debated rivalry between you and Dumont, would you say that the recent shut in you've imposed on yourself, staying out of the media, away from parties or gallery openings, concerts, have you done this to make it easier on the team?"

Roman's heart pounded. The reporter was right. He'd isolated himself from the media and many of the other players, insisting he needed to focus. He'd essentially cut himself off from the world, choosing to spend the summer at his ranch outside of Dallas. In fact, it was a ranch he had never been to before last summer, but he'd only returned to Dallas in time to start training with the team. He'd taken a commuter plane back and forth, actually taking lessons and learning how to fly. But how could he answer that he didn't give a darn about making anything easier on anyone, except himself. His motivation for shutting himself off from the media had only been for one purpose, to try to get Katie out of his mind.

She'd tried to call, and he'd deleted all of her messages. He didn't want to listen to her and think about how much he'd been hurt.

"You know I don't talk to the press anymore." He tried not to get heated up. He focused on the field.

"I'm sorry, Mr. Young. I know that's the rumor, but there's a new rumor that has just leaked about a Katie Winters."

This spiked his blood pressure. He flung to face the reporter. "What?" The thought of her being lambasted in the press was not something that he took lightly.

The reporter pushed on. "It was leaked via a twitter picture." She held up her phone and showed Roman the picture of him and Katie on top of the sledding hill, her pink pom pom hat and his big, stupid grin. "The tweet simply says, 'Come home, QB.' Can you explain that, sir?"

Something surged within his breast. Chills rushed through him. He grinned, and unexpectedly he felt the very core of him that had been angry and heartbroken lighten.

"Mr. Young, can you tell us what this means? And who is Katie Winters?"

He had to blink, and the electricity of the stadium pierced him. He felt more ready to play this game than ever before in his entire life.

"Sir? Are you okay?"

He took the microphone and pointed at the camera. "I'm coming, boss. After we win this game, I'll be there."

CHAPTER 20

THIS TIME THERE WAS NO COLD, icy, and expensive cab ride to Wolfe Creek. He'd rented his own car and took his time up the canyon. After rolling down the windows, he'd basked in the end of summer sunshine, the changing leaves, and the floral scent of the air.

It didn't surprise him to pull up to the Alaskan Inn and see a fresh coat of paint on the rugged cabin's sign. The trees that hovered around the walls were trimmed, and there were roses lining the path to the front door.

He waited outside the door, his heart pounding. He had a gift for her in a bag he clutched to his side. He'd made a special stop after the airport to get it for her.

It didn't feel right to use the doorbell. After all, the place did belong to him. Taking the key out of his pocket, he let himself in, wanting a chance to see it before he went to her.

Even though he'd seen the receipts that had come showing the expenses for updating and maintaining the place, he'd had no idea it would look this good. The whole place had been painted light grey. It had lightened the whole place up, making it feel more welcoming. Even though the rustic feel of the cabin had been kept as part of the décor, there were also new furnishings. A wrap around large, deep brown, leather couch. The fireplace had been redone with a red brick that trailed all the way up to the ceiling. It looked grand. He noted that the civil war rifle was now in a glass case.

His eyes swept across the red accented horseshoes that hung above all the doors. When he saw the new black dining table with a centerpiece of a steel Destroyers emblem in the middle, he closed his eyes as too many emotions hit him at once.

It was perfect. If he were designing a home, a place to have a family and a life, it would have looked exactly like this.

The place was better than he'd imagined it could be.

He walked over and pressed his finger to the cowboy emblem.

Without warning, she came flying through the flip door that separated the kitchen from the main room.

The moment went to a full stop.

Her red hair was down, and soft fluffy curls framed her face. Her green cat eyes instantly filled with moisture, and her lips tugged up. She wore a teal silk tank top and a white skirt with flip-flops. Even though she looked more formal than he'd ever seen her, she still looked fresh, young, and innocent. Just as he'd dreamt of her. But she was the summer version. She let out a breath. "Well."

The fact that his heart almost exploded didn't surprise him. What surprised him was that seeing her again made his tongue feel like he couldn't move it and his palms sweaty.

Staring at her, all he knew was that he never wanted to try to get her out of his head again. Finally, he lifted the bag and grinned. "I guess I should be grateful you don't have a gun pointed at my head this time."

Hesitantly, she took a step toward him, taking the bag. "What's this?" She opened the box inside, pulling out the lemon lotion.

"Just in case you were out," he said quietly. It had been one of many things that had tortured him about her.

She grinned. "Thank you. I almost was."

They both paused, and then he pushed back, nodding to the walls. "It looks great."

She studied him. "Do you think so?"

"It's perfect." He tugged out the folded piece of paper in his pocket and handed it to her.

She took the paper. "What is this?"

"An ad I took out to market the place."

Slowly, the side of her lip lifted and her eyes flashed back to him. "You did?"

"Well, I told you I would."

She hesitated, then put the lotion on the table. "Why didn't you sell it, Roman?"

The way all her vulnerability showed in her eyes made his heart speed up. "Because someone told me once that I should keep a rifle just because it belonged to my Uncle Jim." He shrugged. "Uncle Jim gave me this place, and after some thought, that felt like it should be important to me, too."

Slowly, she nodded. Then she smiled. "Good game yesterday."

It had been a good game. He'd felt on fire, like nothing could stop him. After four touchdowns by half time, the other team had pretty much felt the same way. The Destroyers had stomped them, 38-7. His heart felt even fuller, knowing that she'd watched. "Thanks." He folded his arms. "Why did you tweet that picture?"

One shoulder lifted. "You wouldn't answer my calls. I felt like if I wanted to compete with the other bachelorettes, I had to pull out all my tricks."

"Are you competing?" The memory of her and Lou had been burned into his brain.

Red moved up her neck. The blush settled nicely onto her cheeks. "I guess so."

"Even though you think I should have quit playing football?" He had tortured himself with his decision to sign another contract with the Destroyers.

The center of her brow creased. "If you're asking if I no longer think the sport is by it's very essence dangerous...the answer is no. Of course it's dangerous." Biting the side of her lip, she shook her head. "But I finally realized that life is dangerous. In one moment you can get in a car wreck. In one moment you can find out you have cancer." She sucked in a breath. "But you can't quit living your life. You can't quit doing what you were born to do."

"You think I was born to do this?"

She smirked. "Don't get a big head, QB."

Watching the way her eyes went into cat-like slits as she teased him, he grinned. "I guess you decided not to marry Lou?"

She scoffed. "You're being ridiculous."

He couldn't stop himself. "I saw you kissing him. Right after ..." he hesitated, feeling like a dork, but he said it anyway, "Right after we'd been kissing." It felt so high school. This is what she could reduce him to.

Shaking her head, she smiled.

He sputtered, "What are you smiling about?"

"You're jealous. The bachelor is jealous."

He closed the distance between them, easily linking their fingers together. "Darn right I was jealous," he whispered, and nervous flutters filled his gut.

"No," she corrected. "You are jealous."

He looked up at her. "You have history with him. I can't compete with that."

"You were married to a super model."

He dropped her hand. "I don't want a super model."

A slow smile filled her face. She re-laced their fingers. "Good, cause I don't want Lou."

His heart kicked up a notch. Unable to stop himself, he looked at her lips. "What do you want, Katie?"

"I wanted to know I could count on you. I wanted to know that you wanted this inn. I thought that you wanted it."

"I did want it...I do want it."

She shook her head. "But you were going to sell it."

He tightened his hand on hers. "I was. And I'm sorry. I decided not to, but I hadn't let Mr. Burcher in on the new plan." He put his other hand to his chest. "And I take responsibility for that. It was selfish. I wasted other people's efforts and time on my behalf." He felt the raw emotion bubble inside him. "I'm sorry, Katie. I never meant...to hurt you."

She blinked, and the side of her lip tugged up. "I wanted to quit working for you. I almost did, but do you know what changed my mind?"

Honestly, he'd thought she would quit. He'd been confused when his accountant told him that he'd gotten a bunch of expenses and had asked if he wanted to approve her time card. "What?"

"Mrs. K."

Nervously, he looked down. "Oh, how is she?"

Releasing his hand, she took his face into her hands. Tears burned in her eyes. "Did you know that some anonymous donor paid for the cancer treatments she needed?"

He couldn't stop his own eyes from filling, thinking about how relieved he'd been to hear that the experimental treatments had been working for her. "I'm really happy for her."

She grinned and leaned forward, softly touching her lips to his.

A new kind of energy surged into him, the same kind he'd felt before the big game last night. He drew her closer, pulling his arms around her, deepening the kiss. Her lips had haunted him for months.

"You are a good man, Roman Young." She whispered against his lips.

Not confirming or denying anything, he softly kissed her again. "Well, that's debatable."

Rolling her eyes, she gave him a gentle shove. "If you wouldn't have been all Neanderthalish and left in a blaze of glory, you could have heard me explain how Lou had slammed his mouth against mine without asking."

Hearing that made him burn. His whole body tightened.

"Don't do that."

"What?"

"Get all territorial."

"I wasn't."

"Yes, you were."

He released her and stepped back, trying to clear his head. He'd thought … he'd thought that Katie had been playing him … or … but he knew at this moment that she was telling him the truth. Still, he couldn't stop himself. "I really do love that picture you posted. I haven't been able to stop looking at it."

She scoffed and tried to pull away. "Are you getting a big head, cause I'm still going to make you work for it."

He laughed and pulled her closer, slipping a hand into his pocket. He pulled out a small box. "Believe me, I came ready to work for it." He held the box out to her.

Tears filled her eyes and she gasped. "Oh my goodness."

Her reaction made his eyes fill up, too. "I figure we've been apart long enough that if we haven't moved on, maybe we weren't meant to."

She laughed and opened the box, pulling out the two-carat diamond ring. "Are you sure?"

He dropped to one knee. "So what do you say, boss, will you take the last rose? Then you can boss me around for the rest of my life?"

She sniffed and laughed again, nodding. "Only if you don't cry when I beat you in skiing."

He stood and took the ring, slipping it onto her finger and then lightly kissing her. "Deal."

"So this is the last play?"

"The play that will eventually lead me to victory, yes." He dove in for another kiss.

Giggling, she kissed him back. "You to victory?"

He crushed her in a full hug and lifted her up. "This is the one where I'll take you and run past the goal posts and spike you for the touchdown."

More giggling. "Oh, let's wait for Josh. He loves this kind of stuff."

He put her down. "Okay, how about I just kiss you then."

"Okay."

They kissed until both of them had to come up for air.

He laughed. "And just so you know. I love you, Katie Winters."

Softly, she put her hand to his cheek and peered back into his eyes. "Whether it's the first play or the last, I love you, too, QB."

ABOUT THE AUTHOR

Taylor Hart has always been drawn to a good love triangle, hot chocolate and long conversations with new friends. Writing has always been a passion that has consumed her dreams and forced her to sit in a trance for long hours, completely obsessed with people that don't really exist. Taylor would have been a country star if she could have carried a tune—maybe in the next life. Find Taylor at:

www.taylorhartbooks.com | Twitter:@taylorfaithhart | Facebook: Taylor Hart

Made in United States
Orlando, FL
10 January 2024

42366395R00091